“MILLIONS BUY JACKIE COLL[illegible]S . . . IMPOSSIBLE TO PUT DOWN.”

—*The Wall Street Journal*

“JACKIE COLLINS PULLS OUT ALL THE STOPS, WITH A STRONG VEIN OF SUSPENSE . . . YOU’LL HAVE A MARVELOUS TIME.”

—*Washington Post*

“COLLINS’ GREATEST HALLMARK IS THAT SHE IS A VIRTUAL GEYSER OF NARRATIVE ENERGY . . . JACKIE COLLINS IS ONE OF POPULAR FICTION’S GREATEST NATURAL RESOURCES . . . SHE IS . . . THE UNDISPUTED SCHEHERAZADE OF THE STARS.”

—*New York Post*

Jackie Collins

"NOBODY DOES IT LIKE JACKIE COLLINS . . . "

—*Daily Nebraskan* (Lincoln)

"JACKIE COLLINS POSSESSES A RAZOR-SHARP SENSE OF PACING . . . "

—*Philadelphia Inquirer*

"COLLINS' DEVOTEES WILL . . . RELISH THE SNAPPY DIALOGUE, WHIRLWIND PACING, IRREVERENT HUMOR AND OPULENT LOCALES THAT ARE HER TRADEMARKS."

—*Publishers Weekly*

Jackie Collins

"JACKIE COLLINS' BOOKS ARE HOT AND STEAMY . . . ENOUGH OVERHEATED SEX AND ACTION [TO PUT] POLAR ICE CAPS IN DANGER OF MELTDOWN."

—*Houston Post*

"JACKIE COLLINS' NOVELS ARE ALWAYS GROUNDED IN TRUTH, LACED WITH A BRACING SHOT OF HUMOR . . . MOST IMPORTANTLY, COLLINS IS A GOOD STORYTELLER . . . "

—*Los Angeles Herald-Examiner*

"JACKIE COLLINS IS AT THE TOP OF THE HEAP . . . "

—*Providence Sunday Journal*

Jackie Collins

Books by Jackie Collins

Lady Boss*
Rock Star*
Hollywood Husbands*
Lucky*
Hollywood Wives*
Chances
Lovers and Gamblers
The World Is Full of Divorced Women
The Love Killers*
Sinners*
The Bitch*
The Stud
The World Is Full of Married Men*

* Published by POCKET BOOKS

Jackie Collins

The Love Killers

POCKET BOOKS
New York London Toronto Sydney Tokyo Singapore

This book is a work of fiction. Names, characters, places and incidents are either the product of the author's imagination or are used fictitiously. Any resemblance to actual events or locales or persons, living or dead, is entirely coincidental.

Originally published in a different form as *Lovehead*.

Jewelry courtesy of Tallarico Precious Jewels, Beverly Hills.

POCKET BOOKS, a division of Simon & Schuster Inc.
1230 Avenue of the Americas, New York, NY 10020

ISBN: 0-671-73786-4

First Pocket Books printing April 1989

14 13 12 11 10 9 8 7 6

POCKET and colophon are registered trademarks of Simon & Schuster Inc.

Printed in the U.S.A.

The Love Killers

Chapter 1

"I don't care if you can't do anything else. I don't care if you lose your income, your home, your possessions. Fuck all of it, baby. Just gather up your self-respect and walk right out. To be a prostitute is to be nothing, a mere tool of man. Take no notice of your pimps, your bosses. *We* will help you. *We* will give you all the help we can. *We* will get you so together that your old life will seem like a bad dream."

Margaret Lawrence Brown had been speaking for fifteen minutes, and she paused to sip from a glass of water handed to her on the makeshift podium. The crowd gathered to hear her talk was gratifyingly large. They occupied a vast area of Central Park, mostly women, a few men scattered among them. It was a warm August day in 1974, and her followers had turned out in force.

Margaret's tone was strong and outright. Her voice didn't falter. Her message came across loud and clear.

She was a tall woman in her early thirties. No makeup decorated her strong, radiant face. Her hair was long and black, and she wore denims, boots, and love beads.

Margaret Lawrence Brown was a cult figure in America. A ceaseless campaigner for women's rights, she had won many a victory. She had written three books, appeared on television regularly, and made a great deal of money, all of which she used for her organization, F.W.N.—Free Women Now.

Everyone had laughed when she'd first taken up the cause of the prostitutes. But they weren't laughing now, not after three months, not after thousands of women appeared to be giving up their chosen profession and following her.

"You've got to get it together *now!*" Margaret yelled, a determined thrust to her chin.

"Yeah!" the women yelled back.

"You're going to live again. You're going to come alive!"

"Yeah! Yeah!" The reaction from the crowd was gospel in its intensity.

"You're going to be *free!*" she promised them.

"Yeah!"

Margaret slumped to the ground while the crowd continued to stamp and shout its approval. Blood spurted from a small, neat hole in the middle of her forehead.

It was minutes before the crowd realized what had happened, before hysteria and panic set in.

Margaret Lawrence Brown had been shot.

The house in Miami could only be approached by passing through electric gates, and then undergoing the scrutiny of two uniformed guards with pistols stuck casually in their belts.

Alio Marcusi passed this scrutiny easily. He was a fat old man, with liquid booze-filled eyes and the walk of a pregnant cat.

As he approached the big house he began humming softly to himself, uncomfortable in his too-tight gray-check suit, sweating from the heat of a cloudless day.

A maid answered his ring at the door. A surly, big-limbed Italian girl, she spoke little English, but she nodded at Alio and told him that Padrone Bassalino was out by the pool.

He patted her on the ass, making his way

through the house to the patio that led out to a kidney-shaped swimming pool.

Mary Ann August greeted him. Mary Ann was an exceptionally pretty young woman, with old-fashioned, teased blond hair, and a curvaceous body exhibited in a skimpy polka-dot bikini.

"Hi, there, Alio," she said with a giggle, rising from her lounge. "I was just gonna make myself a little drinkie. Want one?" Posing provocatively in front of him, she toyed with a gold chain hanging between her generous breasts.

Alio contemplated the young vision, licking his lips in anticipation of the day—not far off, surely—when Enzio would grow tired of Mary Ann and pass her on, like all the others.

"Yeah, I'll have a Bacardi, plenty of ice. And some potato chips, mixed nuts, an' a few black olives." He rubbed his extended stomach sorrowfully. "I had no time for lunch. Such a busy day. Where's Enzio?"

Mary Ann gestured out toward the never-ending gardens. "He's around somewhere—pruning his roses, I think," she said sweetly.

"Ah, yes, his roses." Instinctively Alio glanced back at the house, and sure enough, there she was, Rose Bassalino herself, peering out through a narrow chink in her curtains.

Rose, Enzio's wife. She hadn't left her room for years, and the only people she would talk to were her three sons. Rose kept an endless vigil at her window just waiting and watching. It gave Alio the creeps. He didn't know how Enzio stood it.

Mary Ann swayed over to the bar and began preparing drinks. She was nineteen years old and had lived with Enzio Bassalino for almost six months—something of a record, for Enzio never kept them around long.

Settling into a chair, Alio slowly closed his eyes. Such a very busy day . . .

"Hey, ciao, Alio, my friend, my boy. How you feeling?"

Alio awoke with a start and guiltily jumped up.

Enzio loomed over him. Sixty-nine years old, but with the hard, bronzed body of a man half his age, all his own teeth, a craggy, lined face, topped by a mass of thick steel-gray hair.

"I feel good, Enzio, I feel fine," Alio said quickly. They clasped hands, patted each other on the back. They were cousins; Alio owed everything he had to Enzio.

"Can I fix you a drinkie, sweetie-pie?" Mary Ann asked, gazing at Enzio adoringly.

"No." He dismissed her with a look. "Go in the house. I'll ring if I need you."

Mary Ann didn't argue; she obeyed him at once. Perhaps that was why she had lasted longer than the others.

As soon as she was gone Enzio turned to his cousin. "Well?" he asked impatiently.

"It is done," Alio replied in a low voice. "I saw it myself. A masterful job. One of Tony's boys. He vanished before anyone knew what happened. I flew straight here."

Enzio nodded thoughtfully. "There is no greater satisfaction than a perfect hit. This Tony's boy, pay him an extra thousand an' watch him. A man like that could get himself promoted. A public execution is never easy."

"No, it's not," Alio agreed, sucking on a black olive.

"She must be thirty," the woman hissed spitefully.

"Or older," her friend agreed.

Lined, and overly made up, the two middle-aged women watched Lara Crichton climb out of the Marbella Club pool.

Lara was a perfectly beautiful woman of twenty-six. Slim, suntanned, with rounded, sensual breasts, a mane of sun-streaked hair, and wide, crystal-clear green eyes.

She dropped down on the mat next to Prince Alfredo Masserini and sighed loudly. "I'm getting bored with this place," she said restlessly. "Can't we go somewhere else?"

Prince Alfredo sat up. "Why are you bored?" he demanded. "Am *I* boring you? Why should you be bored when you are with me?"

Lara sighed again. Yes, the truth of the matter was the prince could be very boring indeed.

But who else was there? She'd made it a rule never to let go of anyone until there was someone else firmly ensconced in his place. She had been through most of the available princes and counts, a few movie stars, and a lord or two. It really was tiresome she had set herself such high standards.

"I don't understand you," Prince Alfredo complained. "No woman has ever told me she was bored with me. I am *not* a boring man. I am vibrant, lively. I am—how you say—the life and brains of the party."

Lara noticed with an even heavier sigh that as he spoke he was getting an erection in his nifty Cerruti shorts.

"Oh, God, do shut up," she muttered under her breath. Sex was becoming the biggest bore of all. So predictable, worked out, and mechanical.

Prince Alfredo did not hear her. "Come, my darling." Aware of his erection, and proud, he pulled her to her feet. "First we take a rest." He winked slyly. "And then we drive the Ferrari into the mountains. What do you think, my lovely?"

"Whatever you say." Reluctantly she allowed herself to be led inside. All eyes followed them as they left. They certainly made a beautiful and exciting couple.

They had separate suites, but by unspoken agreement all sexual activity took place in

Lara's. She stopped him from entering at the door.

"What's the matter?" he asked indignantly. "I have a good hard-on—a *very* good one."

"Save it for later," she said firmly, closing the door on his protests. "I'll call you when I wake up."

Lara felt restless and hemmed in. A feeling she had often felt when married to Jamie P. Crichton. A divorce had solved the feeling then, but what now?

The phone rang and she picked it up, ready to tell Alfredo no—definitely no. But it was not the prince. The operator informed her it was an urgent call from New York.

"Yes?" She cradled the receiver, wondering who knew she was in Spain.

"Lara? Lara, is that you? Oh, God! This is such a terrible connection." It was a woman's voice, her tone bordering on hysterical.

"Who is this?" Lara asked sharply.

"God! Can't you hear me? Goddamn it—this is Cass." A pause, then, "Lara, something terrible has happened. Margaret's been shot. They've shot Margaret."

Chapter 2

Margaret Lawrence Brown was rushed to the nearest hospital. She was still alive, but only barely.

Her loyal followers gathered in tight, silent groups. Only those closest to her were allowed inside the hospital, where they waited with as much hope as they could muster. There were no tears; Margaret would have hated that.

Cass Long and Rio Java stood together near the door of the emergency room. A doctor had just announced they were doing a blood transfusion.

Cass was Margaret's personal assistant and confidante. They had met in college and been best friends ever since. Cass was a short, untidy-looking woman, with cropped brown hair and a cheerful disposition. Right now her regular features were frozen in shock.

Rio Java—Margaret's most famous supporter, one of her closest friends, and also a staunch and founding member of F.W.N.—was a far more glamorous figure. Undisputed queen of the underground movies, she was a notorious public personality, fashion freak, mother of four children of various colors, and quite outrageous. Over six feet tall, she was starvation-thin, with a long, dramatic face, shaved eyebrows, and exotic makeup. Part Cherokee Indian and part Louisiana hillbilly, she lived her life exactly as she pleased.

"Where's Dukey?" she asked, groping for a cigarette in her oversized purse.

"He's on his way," Cass replied. "And I reached Lara. She's flying in."

They watched silently as more doctors appeared and hurried into the emergency room.

"Can I at least see her?" Cass pleaded, catching one doctor as he emerged.

"Are you a relative?" he asked sympathetically, noting her blood-soaked dress. She had cradled Margaret's head on her lap until the ambulance arrived and then traveled to the hospital with her.

"Yes," Cass lied.

The doctor drew her aside. "It's not a pretty sight," he warned.

She bit her lip. "I know," she whispered. "I brought her in."

The doctor felt sorry for her. "Well, I suppose if you're a relative," he said. "It's against regulations, but—all right, come with me."

Rio nodded at Cass to go ahead, and she followed the doctor into the emergency room.

A team of professionals were doing everything they could. Two catheters were allowing the first pint of blood to be transfused. A tube was at Margaret's nose. A doctor worked at massaging her heart.

Cass felt sick. "There's not much hope, is there?" she asked, choking back tears.

Grimly the doctor shook his head and led her quietly out.

Rio looked at her. They didn't need words, they both knew.

"Who did it?" Cass demanded, rubbing her eyes. She had been asking the same question ever since the fateful moment in the park when Margaret fell. Margaret had so many enemies; a lot of people hated her because of the causes she fought for. *And* because she led her life exactly as she pleased, and didn't give a damn about criticism or gossip. The man she was currently living with was Dukey K. Williams, a black soul singer with a dubious past. Cass didn't like him. She felt he was using Margaret to get publicity for his sagging career.

Rio dragged deeply on her cigarette. "Listen —it's no secret Margaret made enemies. It comes with the territory. She knew it."

"I kept on warning her," Cass replied mournfully. "She never listened. Margaret never thought anything through, she just went for it."

"Ah, yes," Rio replied. "But that's what makes her so special, isn't it?"

"I guess," Cass said, thinking about all the hate mail Margaret received. "Nigger Lover," "Commie Bitch," and the like. There were also threats to kill her. "Lawrence Brown. I saw you on 'The Tonight Show.' I hate you. I hope you drop dead. I might kill you myself."

These letters were almost a daily occurrence, so mundane as to be casually deposited in the lunatic file and forgotten.

The ones that always worried Cass were the telephone threats. Muffled voices warning Margaret to leave certain causes alone. Recently it had been the matter of the prostitutes. So many had been following Margaret, that suddenly the pimps, the madams, and the hoods that controlled it all were getting worried. A dearth of prostitutes—it was becoming an impossible situation, and each time Margaret held one of her open-air rallies hundreds more vanished overnight, spurred on by the fact that F.W.N. offered them more than words; it offered them a chance of starting afresh. The organization arranged jobs, living accommodations, even money if the need was urgent.

There had been many threats for Margaret to drop the "Great Hooker Revolution," as *New Month* magazine called it. They had recently featured her on their cover with a six-page story inside. But Margaret had no intention of dropping anything. Margaret Lawrence Brown was fearless when it came to her causes.

Dukey K. Williams rushed to the hospital from a recording session. There was a struggle to get inside—the place was swarming with police, press, and television crews.

Dukey, accompanied by his manager and P.R. man, refused any comment as he pushed his way through the mob. At the elevator he was stopped by a security guard who refused to allow him to board.

"Jesus Christ!" Dukey screamed his frustration. "Get this lowlife outta my way before I fuckin' cream him."

The guard glared, his hand twitching nervously near his gun.

"Calm down, Dukey." His manager tried to defuse the situation. "They're only protecting Margaret. Cass must be up there."

Cass was sent for, and the guard allowed Dukey and his entourage through.

"Jesus Christ! How did it happen?" Dukey

demanded. "Have they caught the son of a bitch who did it? Will she make it? What the *fuck* is goin' on?"

Sadly Cass shook her head. "They don't seem to know," she replied quietly. "It doesn't look good."

Rio was at the elevator to meet them. "Forget it," she said in a flat, toneless voice. "Margaret just died."

Chapter 3

Enzio Bassalino was a big and powerful man with huge shoulders and a wide girth. It always amused Mary Ann August when the mood took him to cook dinner. He would clear the kitchen of all the help, tie an apron around his waist, and then go to work cooking spaghetti, his special meat sauce à la Enzio, and hearty chunks of garlic bread.

"Honey—you look so *funny* in that apron," Mary Ann trilled. She was allowed in the kitchen only as long as she promised not to interfere. "Don't you want Little Mama to help you?"

Little Mama was the nickname Enzio used

for her. She was unaware of the fact it had also been the pet name of every girl before her.

"No." He shook his head. "What you can do, Little Mama, is you can bring me some more vino. Pronto!"

Mary Ann obliged and then perched on the edge of the kitchen table, swinging her long legs back and forth. She was wearing an extremely tight dress cut very low in front. Enzio chose her clothes, and they were always of the same style. She was not allowed to wear pants, shirts, or anything casual. Enzio liked her to look sexy.

Mary Ann didn't mind. Life was certainly a lot better with Enzio than it had been before, and she catered to his every need. After all, Enzio Bassalino was a very important man, and she was thrilled and honored to be with him.

"Taste this." Proudly he offered her a spoonful of the steaming, rich meat sauce.

Dutifully she opened her mouth. "Ouch, Noonzi, it's hot!" She pouted. "You've burned your Little Mama."

Enzio roared with laughter. He was celebrating. Tonight he would laugh at anything.

"Sometimes you're really nasty." Mary Ann lapsed into baby talk. "Why you so mean to your rickle lickle girlie?"

"Ha!" he said with a snort. "You don't even

know what mean is." He dipped his finger in the bubbling sauce, licked it approvingly, and added more wine. "You're a cute girl," he said condescendingly. "Stay that way and you'll be all right. Okay, Little Mama?"

She giggled happily. "Okay, Big Daddy."

In his own peculiar way he was quite fond of Mary Ann. She was dumber than most broads and never asked any questions. She was also stacked just the way he liked, and obliging. Nothing was ever too much trouble.

Enzio hated the usual routine. They moved in, and within weeks they thought they owned you. Broads! They asked questions, got nosy, and sometimes had the nerve to plead a headache when he wanted to make love. Enzio was very proud of the fact that even now, aged sixty-nine, he could still get it up once or twice a week. Often he thought about the times when it was once, twice, or even three or four times a night. What a stud he had been! What a magnificent stallion!

Now it was up to his sons to carry on the Bassalino tradition with women. And he had three of them, three fine young men of whom he was more than proud. They were his life. Through them the name of Bassalino would remain a force to be reckoned with. And when he became old, really old, they would be there to protect him as he had protected them.

It was a good job they had not taken after their mother. Rose was crazy, as far as Enzio was concerned, locked up in her room, spying, only speaking to her sons when they visited. She had been there for seventeen years. Ah . . . seventeen years of trying to break his balls, trying to make him feel the guilt.

But her little game hadn't worked with him. He refused to feel guilty about anything. Let *her* be the one to suffer. It was all her fault anyway. What he did was his business, and she had no right to interfere.

In his heyday Enzio Bassalino had acquired the nickname of The Bull. This was on account of his habit of mounting every agreeable female who crossed his path. One day, while dallying with the wife of a friend of his known as Vincent the Hog, he'd received his one and only bullet wound. "Right up the ass," the story went. "Vincent the Hog caught them at it and shot him right up the ass."

Fortunately for Enzio that story wasn't strictly true. Vincent the Hog had shot him, all right, but the bullet had landed in a fleshy part of his posterior and not caused any real damage. All the same, Enzio was hardly pleased. After the incident Vincent the Hog had suffered a series of mishaps beginning with his house burning down and ending with his being fished out of the river on the other end of a concrete block.

Enzio did not take kindly to ridicule, and the story of his being shot had caused many an unwelcome snigger.

Shortly after that he met and married Rose Vacco Morano, the daughter of a friend. She was slim and proud-faced, with the fragile Madonna quality of a young Italian virgin. Enzio was smitten the first time he saw her and wasted no time in asking her to marry him. It didn't take him long to plan an elaborate wedding. Rose wore white lace, and Enzio a shiny black morning suit, white shoes, gloves, and a red carnation. He figured he looked pretty dapper.

On their wedding day Rose was just eighteen and Enzio thirty-three.

They became a popular couple, Rose soon shrugging off her quiet upbringing and joining in the more flamboyant life-style of her husband. She had no desire to become a housewife, stay at home, and involve herself in cooking, children, and church activities. When she dutifully gave birth to their first son, Frank, the baby was left at home with a nanny while Rose continued to spend all her time out and about with Enzio. Rose Bassalino was a woman born before her time.

Enzio didn't mind; in fact, he was delighted. His wife was turning into a beautiful, smart woman, and Enzio knew he was much envied.

While other men left their wives at home and took their girlfriends to the racetracks, bars, and clubs, Enzio brought Rose. She became one of the boys, their friend and confidante, and everyone loved her.

Enzio often marveled at his luck in finding such a gem. Rose satisfied him in every way and even found time to present him with a second son, Nick, three years after the birth of Frank.

What a woman! Enzio kept no secrets from her. She knew all about his business activities, and as he grew more successful, took over more territory, knocked out more rivals, she was right there helping him. On more than one occasion she was at his side when he dealt out his particular form of justice to people who had double-crossed him. "My Rose has more balls than most men," he proudly boasted. "She's one fine woman."

Nobody argued.

Rose had many admirers, and Enzio knew it. It puffed him up with pride. She was *his* wife, and nothing could change that.

When Angelo, their third son, was born, Rose finally decided she should spend more time at home. Frank was twelve and Nick nine, and they needed attention. Enzio agreed. There was no point in her accompanying him on the short trips to Chicago and the Coast. Now they had a beautiful mansion on Long Island, and it was only right that Rose should spend more time with the children and enjoy it.

She persuaded him that maybe they should enlarge their circle of friends, as, after all, most of the people they saw were involved in the rackets, and Rose thought it might be a good idea to have a different group around for a change. There was an actor and his wife who owned an estate close by, and soon Rose started inviting them over. A banking family came next, and then Charles Cardwell, a cash-poor snob who lingered at the bottom of high society. Gradually Rose surrounded them with new people, until eventually all the old faces were squeezed out.

By the time Enzio decided he didn't like it, it was too late. His business trips became longer; he acquired a small apartment in New York, plus a stream of whorish girlfriends. "Dumbheads," he called them. He still adored Rose, but she had changed, and he couldn't understand why.

One night he returned home hours before she expected him. He wanted to surprise her; it was the week of their twenty-first wedding anniversary, and he thought they might talk, try to work things out. He wanted to explain how he wasn't happy. Maybe make an attempt to recapture the closeness they'd once shared.

At thirty-nine Rose was still a fiercely attractive woman. Her hair was a thick swirl of bluish-black, her dark complexion unlined, and her figure the same girlish shape he had married.

She greeted him coldly. "I want a divorce," she said. "I'm going to marry Charles Cardwell. I know about your apartment, your street whores, and I want to be free of you."

Enzio listened in amazement. Charles Cardwell was twenty-six years old, his parents had money, but he had a long wait before he inherited a dime.

Enzio was calm. "Have you slept with him?" he asked. "Yes," Rose replied defiantly. She never lied. The woman didn't know what fear was.

Enzio nodded thoughtfully and agreed to her requests. Satisfied, she went to bed.

For a while he sat in his favorite armchair and gazed into space. Eventually he made some phone calls, and later that night Charles Cardwell was brought to the house.

He was a pale young man, obviously shaken and frightened of his escort—four of Enzio's most trusted lieutenants. He smiled weakly at Enzio. "Now listen," he began. "Let me explain—"

Enzio ordered his mouth taped, his arms and legs tied.

They carried him up to Rose's bedroom like a side of beef.

She awoke with a start and stared at the

helpless figure of her lover. Then her eyes shifted to Enzio. Despairingly she shook her head, well aware of her husband's brand of justice.

He took her from the bed and held her so she couldn't move, only watch. And then the knives came out.

Charles Cardwell was sliced to death in front of her.

Chapter 4

It was not easy for Lara to extract herself from the prince. They had been together constantly for six months, and he was possessive, suspicious—and most of all, hotly jealous.

When she told him she had to leave immediately for New York, he jumped to the only conclusion possible for his mind to reach. "Who is he? What has he got to offer you that I cannot give you? I *demand* you tell me his name."

"It's not a man," Lara explained patiently. "It's a family situation."

"But you have no family, Lara, you always told me that," he stated petulantly.

She nodded. "I know, but I do have these distant relatives in America." A pause. "I have a half sister named Beth, and she needs me."

"A half sister!" Prince Alfredo shouted. "You can't just *acquire* a stepsister." He stamped around angrily. "I know it's a man, Lara. I know. You cannot lie to me."

Her mind was on more important things. "Oh, please!" she exclaimed impatiently. "Think what you like. I have to leave, and that's that."

"Then I will come with you."

"I don't want you to."

"I must insist."

"*No,* Alfredo."

"*Yes,* Lara."

They argued some more until at last he left and she was able to finish packing. It was a relief to be rid of him; the man was impossible. Why was she wasting her time?

Lara Crichton always got first-class service wherever she went. Young, gorgeous, the ex-wife of one of the richest men in London, she was truly one of what the press referred to as "the beautiful people." Constantly featured in the glossy fashion magazines as a shining example of jet-set glamour, she epitomized all that Margaret Lawrence Brown was against.

It would have been a journalistic scoop for someone to discover that they were in fact half-sisters, sharing the same father but different mothers.

For individual reasons, as each reached personal fame, they felt no need to reveal the fact to anyone. They had been raised in different countries; their whole lives were completely alien to each other. Occasionally they met, and there was a true warmth between them, a love that crossed their very obvious differences. They understood each other and never criticized the other's way of life.

Their father, Jim Lawrence Brown, had never married either of their mothers. Margaret was five when her mother died, and Jim had moved on, taking the child with him to California. There he met a married woman separated from her husband. Jim and Margaret moved in with her, and eventually the woman gave birth to Lara. A year later, when she and her husband decided to get back together, they gave Jim the child and six thousand dollars to move on again. The money tempted him. He didn't argue.

With the cash he bought an old car and trailer, which served as a sort of home. At seven years of age Margaret was completely in charge of one-year-old Lara.

Jim was a natural drifter; he was always in a dream, playing his guitar, chasing pretty women, or sleeping. He drove them to Arizona, where they stayed on a farm owned by a widow named Mary Chaucer. She took care of Lara and insisted Margaret start school. "The girl is very bright," she told Jim. "Advanced for her years. She must have an education."

After a while Jim began to get restless. He had been far too long in the same place, only now he was tied by two children, and it was a responsibility he wasn't up to. Lara often thought that was why he must have decided to marry Mary Chaucer. She was older than he, a plump, smiling lady who never complained.

Exactly one month after their marriage Jim took off, leaving nothing more than a scrawled note telling Mary to look after his kids.

Margaret was nine. She was the one who found his note. It was a coward's note, full of apologies and five hundred dollars.

Eight months after his departure Mary gave birth to Jim's third daughter, Beth, a child he never even knew existed.

After that things were different. With no man around, work at the farm became slapdash and unorganized. Mary was always tired and sick. The baby wore her out. Money started to run short, as did the once-smiling Mary's temper. Margaret was packed off to boarding school, while Lara was sent to relatives of Mary's in England. They did not see each other again for ten years, by which time Margaret was attending college on a scholarship and Lara was doing well as a teen model in London.

Beth, now ten, lived with Mary in a small apartment. She went to school while Mary worked.

Margaret wanted to help them, but it was hard enough managing to pay for her own education—an education she was determined to have.

At sixteen Lara was quite beautiful, natural, with none of the polish she later acquired. She was happy living in England; in fact, to Margaret she seemed almost completely English—accent and all. They spent a weekend together in New York, and the closeness of their early years was still there.

Time went by and they went their separate, highly individual ways. Occasionally they wrote or phoned. But the need for contact was not there; there was a deeper bond of love and security.

Mary Chaucer died of cancer when Beth was fifteen, and although both her sisters invited her to come and live with them, she preferred a more independent life and went off to a hippie commune with her boyfriend, Max.

Margaret didn't object. She was already launched on an equality-for-women project. Her first book, *Women—The Unequal Sex*, was about to be published. Her star was beginning to shine.

In London Lara met and married Jamie P. Crichton, whose father happened to be one of the richest men in England—and Jamie was his only heir. Unfortunately, their marriage did not last longer than a year, but it was long enough to establish Lara as a personality in her own right. The gossip columns hardly went to press without carrying her picture or some anecdote about what she was wearing or doing, or with whom she had been seen. Lara became the darling of life in the fast lane.

The shooting of Margaret Lawrence Brown made headlines, but the photographers still turned out at Kennedy Airport to welcome Lara Crichton.

She posed briefly in her Yves Saint Laurent suit and big hat, her cool green eyes hidden behind fashionably large sunglasses, Gucci bracelets jangling alongside her black-faced Cartier watch.

"What are you here for, Miss Crichton?" asked an inquisitive reporter.

"Business," she replied, unsmiling. "Personal business."

There was a limousine waiting for her, and with a deep sigh she sat back and tried to relax.

Margaret was dead.

Margaret had been murdered.

Oh, God! Why?

In excruciating detail she remembered her last meeting with her sister. Visiting New York for two days of concentrated shopping, she'd almost skipped phoning her. But then she'd called, and as usual Margaret invited her over. She'd fitted the visit in between lunch at "21" and a hair-streaking session at Vidal's.

Margaret had greeted her in her usual outfit of faded jeans and worn shirt. The perennial blue-tinted shades she wore to help her eyesight covered her eyes, and her long hair was unkempt. Naturally she had no makeup on her striking face.

Lara tut-tutted. "If you bothered," she said, "you could look really ravishing."

Margaret laughed. "Do you realize how much time you waste plastering yourself with stupid crap?" she asked good-naturedly.

"Don't knock it. I'm getting a directorship of a big makeup company," Lara said firmly. "I'll send you a crate of perfumes, lipsticks, glosses, all sorts of things. You'll love it."

"No way, kid!" Margaret replied. "You might think *you* need it. But honey-pie—*I* don't give a damn."

"Well, you should," Lara said primly.

"Says who?"

"Says me."

Margaret smiled. She had a wonderful smile; it lit up a room. "What's happening in your life, baby sister?" she asked, full of warm concern.

Without further prompting Lara launched into a full discussion of what was going on. Margaret fixed her a drink, and they sat down in the cluttered apartment, and she let it all come out. She always did with her sister; it was better than going to an analyst.

Without pause she'd talked about her problems for over an hour. Was Prince Alfredo the one? Should she sell some of her blue-chips? What did Margaret think of her new emerald ring?

Boring small chat. Looking back, Lara shuddered. She'd never asked Margaret about herself. She'd never bothered to discuss any of her sister's burning causes, even though she knew how important they were to her.

How narrow she must have seemed. How selfish and completely involved with herself. And yet Margaret listened patiently, as if she had all the time in the world. She always did.

Why was it you always found out how much you needed someone just when it was too late?

Lara stared out of the window as the limousine headed toward the city. Margaret was dead, and she intended to find out why.

Somebody was going to pay for her sister's death. She would make sure of that.

Chapter 5

Beth Lawrence Brown came to New York by train. It was the first time she had been there. In fact, it was the first time she had been anywhere outside of the commune that had been her home since she was fifteen. Now twenty, she was clear-skinned and fair-haired, with hair that hung straight and thick, reaching below her waist. She was a very pretty girl. Her face had a childlike innocence, with large blue eyes and a wide, soft mouth.

Beth wore her usual outfit, a long dress of Indian fabric, patched in places, thonged sandals on bare feet, and many necklaces of thin leather with hand-painted beads and signs hanging from them. Close to her neck, almost a choker, was a thin gold chain with a gold cross. On the cross were engraved the words LOVE—PEACE—MARGARET.

The two sisters had been very close—not in terms of distance, but in the same way that Lara and Margaret were close. There was a true feeling of unity.

Beth carried with her a large, pouchy suede purse. In it were her things—a hairbrush, a pair of jeans, a flimsy blouse, and many books. She didn't believe in possessions, only books—her passion was reading.

"Wanna buy me a drink, cutie?" A drunk sidled up to her. "I'll give ya a lil' action in exchange."

She ignored him, her expression pensive and thoughtful. Margaret would have told him to fuck off. Lara would have said what a dreadful little man he was. How different her two sisters were.

Cass had promised there would be someone to meet her. She was supposed to wait at the information booth, but the train was early, and she didn't want to hang around, so she decided to walk to Cass's apartment.

She couldn't believe what had happened. It was inconceivable that Margaret was dead. She was such a good person, so clever and bright and caring. So she was tough—everyone knew that—but how else could she have survived?

She hasn't survived, Beth thought sadly. My sister is dead.

Beth had last seen her six months previously. Margaret had arrived to stay for a weekend. Everyone at the commune liked her; in fact, they welcomed her visits. She brought all the new books, record albums, and toys for the children—clever toys, not commercial junk. There were ten children living on the farm, and the responsibility of raising them was shared among the five women and eight men who also lived there. One of the children was Beth's, a little girl of four. Max was her father.

Margaret had greeted her niece, Chyna, with special hugs and kisses. "She's going to grow up to be president one day," she joked. "She's so smart, I love it!"

Beth smiled serenely. "With you to guide her, I'm sure anything is possible."

"Bet on it, kid. When she's ten she's coming to live with me in New York. We'll take it from there."

Margaret shared in the work over the long weekend. She didn't mind what she did—washing floors, helping with the cooking, gardening. She said it helped her relax. She also found time to sit and talk to Beth, listen to her problems, and give advice.

They had a party the night before she left. Great sounds and great hash Max had brought in from California. Margaret had gone off with Clasher because he was short and ugly and the least likely to be her choice. Sex was a very free thing at the commune. There were no hang-ups or jealousies. None of the pressures of life in the real world.

When Margaret left the next morning she had given Beth the gold chain, kissed her, and whispered softly, "You're really lucky. You're doing what you want to do, *and* you're happy. You can't ask for anything more, kid."

And Beth had smiled, a wide, childish smile, and made Margaret promise to come back soon.

"After the summer," Margaret had said. "Maybe for Christmas."

Now the summer was almost ending, and Beth was in New York. She didn't know for how long, but she knew it was where she had to be.

Enzio took the call in his study. He smiled and nodded. Of course, things were back to normal. He had been right. His decision was the only way. Semiretired he might be, but for any major problem that had to be taken care of, he was the one they all turned to.

Frank, his oldest son, had suggested other ways of dealing with the trouble. But what did

Frank know? Thirty-six years old, a good businessman, but when it came to decisions his ideas were all soft. What good were threats if you didn't plan to carry them through?

Definite action like the old days was the only way.

Margaret Lawrence Brown had been dead two weeks, and the trouble had stopped. With no one to guide them, no leader to turn to, the hookers were quiet. It was almost as if the killing of Margaret had killed their fighting spirit. Fuck 'em. Goddamn whores.

Slowly, girls who had disappeared, taken other jobs, came drifting back. They seemed oblivious to the beatings and humiliations they faced. They seemed once more defeated.

Enzio was in a buoyant mood. He called up a furrier friend and ordered a full-length chinchilla coat for Mary Ann. It arrived within hours, and they celebrated on it. Mary Ann was not quite sure what they were celebrating, but she was a willing partner in anything Enzio wished to do.

"You are my great big Italian lover," she purred, knowing that he loved praise. "My big, *big* man."

"And you are one hot, juicy little broad," he replied laughingly. "My favorite tasty slice of lasagna!"

He liked to look at her, the curvy body, big breasts, silky skin, and pouty mouth. It would be quite a while before he grew tired of this one.

Oh, yeah, Enzio Bassalino knew a good piece when it came his way.

Chapter 6

Lola was not the girl's real name. She was thin and scruffy, with city-smoke eyes, and clothes that announced her as the hooker she was. She bit her nails all the time, hungry, addictive little nibbles. Her arms told the story of a heavy drug habit. She was nineteen years old.

Lola had been beaten up. Not badly, a few bruises around her body, cigarette burns on her legs and arms. Just enough to make her aware there was more to come.

She knew all about it. She had known about it before it happened. Lola lived with Charlie

Mailer, and Charlie was one of Tony's boys. Charlie had pulled the hit on Margaret Lawrence Brown.

Lola scurried down the street. It was the first time she'd been out since it happened, the first time she'd dared.

She wore a short skirt, summer lace-up boots, and a tight sweater. Her hair was untidily long, and her eyes were decorated with spiky eyelashes.

Charlie had kicked her out of bed—"Get out and earn something, then maybe we'll catch a movie. An' listen, bitch—don't you come back with less than a coupla hundred, or I'll fuckin' burn your dumb ass."

She'd been huddled in bed for two weeks, and Charlie hadn't minded. Flushed with his own success, he was out celebrating. Tony was pleased with him. Tony wanted him around. And Tony was one of the big guys.

Lola knew Charlie was ready to dump her. He was moving up, and he didn't want her hanging on.

She didn't care. She knew what she had to do.

A man stopped her, pulling her roughly by the arm. She jerked herself free. "Not tonight," she muttered feverishly. "This girl ain't workin' tonight."

She hurried on, occasionally glancing behind her, making sure she wasn't followed.

There was a torn piece of newspaper clutched in her hand, with an address circled in red. Stopping for a moment, she peered at it.

"Where ya goin', girlie?" A passing drunk rolled toward her.

"Piss off," she snapped sharply, hurrying on her way.

When at last she found the circled address she hesitated before going inside. For a while she hovered on the sidewalk, gazing up at the apartment building, thinking about Susie, her little sister. And then suddenly she spat angrily on the pavement and without further ado marched right in.

"I'm here to see . . . uh . . . Cass Long," she told the doorman.

He looked her over, pursed his lips, and indicated the reception desk.

Behind the desk sat a grizzled old man with a sour expression.

"Cass Long," she said.

"She expectin' ya?"

Lola shook her head. "No. You'd better tell her it's urgent."

Leaning forward, his watery eyes stayed fixed on her legs while he buzzed Cass's apartment.

Cass told him to send the girl right up. So many women had been to see her since Margaret's death, she was used to it. She gave them coffee and a picture of Margaret inscribed "Peace—Love." In a way it was a solace to know how deeply so many people had cared. She liked to talk to them.

Putting down the house phone, she said, "There's another one on the way up. Will you let her in?"

Beth nodded. She'd been there a few days, and Cass didn't know how she could have managed without her. Margaret's baby sister had turned out to be strong and loving—a great comfort.

Beth opened the door for Lola and led her into the kitchen to offer refreshments. She knew by the girl's eyes she was a junkie. Life on the commune had not sheltered her from the harder facts of life.

"I don't want anything," Lola said restlessly. "Are you Cass?"

"No," Beth replied quietly.

"Well, like I gotta see Cass. Get her."

Cass came in then. She looked tired. There were deep purple shadows under her eyes; she was having trouble sleeping.

"I got somethin' t'tell you," Lola said hastily. "I don't want no reward, pity, nothin' like that. You can sure see what I am, it's no big secret." She paused to nibble on a hangnail, realized what she was doing, and stopped. "Margaret Lawrence Brown gave people hope. She wouldn't have gotten *me* together—I'm nothin' but a loser. Only I had a sister—just a baby. Aw, *shit*—I can't even tell you what they did to her." She paused again, wiping her nose on the back of her hand. "Anyway—about Margaret. One of Tony's boys made the hit. It don't matter who—he was working on orders. Tony was working on orders, too. The big guy who ordered it done was Enzio Bassalino—*he* arranged it—the hit was *all* his."

"Who's Enzio Bassalino?" Beth asked.

"This big guy prick. He lives in some fancy mansion in Miami. They say he's retired, but believe me—he controls it all. The words to waste her came outta *his* mouth—not out of no gun."

Cass didn't say anything. Intuition told her the girl was speaking the truth.

"Now I told you, I gotta get outta here." Lola stood up and scurried toward the door.

"Wait a minute," Cass said quickly. "If what you're saying is true, let's get the police in on it."

Lola laughed harshly. "Cops. Are you shittin' me? Half of them are in Bassalino's pocket. *Everyone's* on the take. If you want him, you're gonna hafta get him yourself."

"I don't understand," Beth said.

"Yeah, well, think about it. You can do it. You're both clever. You got connections." Lola shivered; she had more to do. "*I'm* gonna take care of the guy who made the hit. Yeah, I'm *really* gonna look after that motherfucker. He's called Charlie Mailer. Remember his name an' watch the papers, you'll be readin' about him." She stopped by the door, a forlorn figure. "Just don't forget who the real murderer is. *Enzio Bassalino.* I admired Margaret Lawrence Brown, an' I wanna be sure you're gonna get that Bassalino bastard."

"Can't you wait?" Cass pleaded. She wanted to call Dukey or Rio, someone who would understand this whole thing better than she and Beth did.

Lola shook her head. "I gotta split. I've told you enough."

Outside it was dark, and Lola headed for Times Square. She didn't have to pull a trick or make a score, but somehow it seemed right that she did.

Stationing herself in the foyer of a movie house, she approached the first man going in on his own.

He was middle-aged, with a throaty cough. They bargained and then walked briskly to his nearby hotel. He insisted on entering first, alone, and she followed a few minutes later.

His room was small and poky, the bed unmade. Lola began to undress, and the man told her to keep her boots on. He took nothing off, merely unzipped his trousers and shook himself free.

They started to have sex. Lola stared unseeingly at the ceiling. She was calm and detached; she knew exactly what she was going to do.

He finished quickly, and Lola took her money and left. She walked slowly home.

Charlie was asleep. She went into the kitchen, stared into the fridge, took out a can of Coke, opened it, and drank straight from the can. The cold bubbles hurt her throat. Then she reached on top of the fridge, groping toward the back where she knew Charlie kept his revolver. Reaching the gun, she checked it carefully. It was loaded.

Lola fitted on the silencer. Living with Charlie had taught her a lot about guns.

Walking to the door of the bedroom, she called out his name.

Charlie awoke slowly. He sat up, rubbing his eyes, and the first thing he saw was Lola pointing a gun at him. "What the fuck—" he began, leaping from the bed.

She shot him in the leg. The bullet made a satisfying soft thud.

His face was a mask of seething fury mixed with surprise. "You dumb cunt!" he yelled.

She shot him between the legs, aiming at his crotch.

He screamed out in agonizing pain.

She didn't hesitate. She shot him in the chest, and he fell to the floor with a heavy thud and was finally silent.

Putting the gun down beside him, she walked out of the apartment, took the elevator to the forty-seventh floor, and let herself out of the fire exit door to the roof.

Determinedly she walked to the edge and without stopping hurled herself over.

Lola was impaled on some spiked railings and died in the ambulance on the way to the hospital.

Chapter 7

The revenge was Rio's idea. They couldn't kill, they weren't murderers, and anyway the man who had pulled the trigger—Charlie Mailer—had been dispatched by Lola with a bullet through the balls. As she'd promised, they read about it in the newspapers, *and* about her own sad suicide.

Rio hired a detective to get them a dossier on Enzio Bassalino. It turned out he was a bad boy—a Mister Big bad boy. He didn't seem to care about anything or anyone. And yet he had three weaknesses—his three sons, Frank, Nick, and Angelo.

If one wanted to hurt Enzio Bassalino, there were three logical ways to go about it.

"It's settled, then?" Rio asked. She stared around at the small gathering in Cass's living room. " 'Cause I don't want *nobody* backing out once we agree. You got it?" She leveled her gaze at Lara. "No getting bored and hightailing off to some hot-shit jet-set paradise."

Lara spoke vehemently, her face flushed. "Listen, Rio, this is no game to me. Margaret was my sister, and different though we may have been, I loved her as much as any one of you." Her green eyes challenged Rio. "I know what I have to do, and believe me, I'll do it very well."

"Rio didn't mean anything," Cass interjected, always one to keep the peace. "We're all uptight. Who wouldn't be after the last few weeks? Now that it's settled and we've decided what we're going to do, I think we'll all breathe easier. I know *I* certainly will."

Dukey K. Williams stood up, his powerful frame menacing the room. "Nobody's goddamn listenin' to me," he complained, "but believe me—*my* way is the right way."

"Your way!" Rio scoffed. "Your way is shit. What do you think? That we can just go up to the dude and say Oh, good morning Mister Big Boss Man Bassalino, I understand it was you who gave the order to shoot Margaret. Well, come on over here, Mister Bad Man, for I am going to beat you to a pulp with my big strong hands." She snorted her disgust. "Dukey, you're full of it. This guy Bassalino is a big-time capo. If you got anywhere near him, you'd get your ass burned good. And even if you *can* get to him—what then? Kill him? Hey, man, what's dead? Dead is nothing. Dead is an easy scene. The way we've thought of is the *only* way to really get to the fucker—*the only way.*"

Dukey glared at her. "Rio, baby, your problem is you live your life between your legs. A little bit of screwin' here, a little bit of ass there. So fuckin' what? These guys have had it all before. Your pussy got a fur lining or somethin'?"

"Fuck you, Dukey. I can make it work," she said confidently.

"Yeah, *you* probably can. A sex freak like you. Maybe Lara, too, I'm not into her whole scene. But Beth? You've gotta be kidding. A baby like her will get mashed up and eaten by the dudes *you're* talkin' about."

Beth spoke up for herself. "I can do it," she said hotly. "I haven't led such a sheltered life. Besides"—she widened her soft, blue eyes—"I want to do it. For Margaret."

"It's settled," Rio announced. "Fucking settled. And we start as soon as possible."

* * *

Dukey K. Williams left the meeting shortly after, muttering under his breath. "Dumb broads. What do they know? Nothin'. Like *nothin'*."

He climbed into his white Rolls Royce, parked illegally outside Cass's building, angrily shoving a tape into the tape deck. It happened to be *Dukey K. Williams Sings Dukey K. Williams*. The first track was "Soul, Grit, and Margaret." He had written it for her.

Jesus Christ, what a stubborn woman she'd been. One hell of a wild lady—in bed *and* out. If only she'd listened to him . . .

"Drop it," he'd warned her time and time again. "Don't fuck with the big boys. So you save a few hookers, it ain't gonna help. Save a few, lose a few, it's all shit."

"What's the matter, Dukey? Don't you think hookers deserve saving?" Margaret had asked.

"Hell, honey—if you do get 'em off the streets, before you can say big bucks they'll be back out again."

"Cynical."

"Cynical—shit, I'm a realist. Give up, babe, it's a losin' proposition."

"That's what everyone told me about you."

"Yeah?"

"Absolutely."

"So why are you with me?"

"Because I looked beyond the image and I

found a man I could relate to. A man who's had his share of tough knocks."

Margaret understood him better than anyone. She had taken the time to find out why he'd been in trouble in the past, and when he'd told her everything about himself she'd stayed with him anyway. And it wasn't just sex. The sex was something else, but what really mattered was not so much the physical action—more a clash of two opposite and very strong personalities bound irrevocably together.

"Do me a favor, babe. Forget about saving any more hookers. Trust me—it's too dangerous," he'd told her.

She had just smiled at him, that warm, sexy Margaret smile, and ignored his advice.

He didn't know how it happened, but suddenly he was in the middle. Right in the fuckin' middle. There was money he owed—not a lot by his standards, a couple of hundred thousand. No big deal, he could pick that up on an album, or a couple of weeks doing a gig in some Las Vegas shithouse. But he owed it, and the way things were, he just didn't have it on hand to pay back. He'd recently had to pay a giant sum to ex-wife number two, and his other expenses were big and immediate. Dukey K. Williams lived as a real duke would have liked to.

So anyway, he owed money to some big boys in Vegas. Of course, they knew he was good for it. Lots of stars lost at the tables before their salaries even hit their pockets; there was nothing unusual about that. The situation was under control.

It was no secret when he started going with Margaret Lawrence Brown. In her own way she was as famous as he was. The newspapers and magazines began discussing their relationship as if they were two slabs of prime steak, not human beings with thoughts and feelings.

At first it was tough, but it didn't seem to bother Margaret, and if it didn't bother her, who was he to complain?

Then she got on her kick about saving the hookers. It wasn't enough she had every little housewife across America up in arms and ready for a revolution. No. She wanted the whores. And when Margaret wanted something, she made sure she got it.

Her campaign was slow and clever, and at first people laughed. Save the hookers! For what?

Dukey was also skeptical. He couldn't help admiring her, but even he didn't believe she was *that* powerful.

But that powerful she was. And suddenly people were not laughing any more, and suddenly Dukey began getting a few calls, and suddenly there he was, right in the fuckin' middle.

"Stop your girlfriend's action and we'll forget

about your debt" was the way the calls started. And as they got heavier and heavier, Dukey tried, *really* tried, to persuade Margaret to stop.

As usual, she didn't want to know. Margaret did things her way.

Eventually he paid off his two-hundred-thousand debt just to get them off his back. He had to borrow the money from a friend out of his past, a narcotics boss named Bosco Sam.

Immediately the threatening calls stopped.

A week later Margaret was shot.

Dukey wanted revenge. He wanted it just as much as Rio and Cass and the two sisters he had known nothing about until after Margaret's murder.

Their plan was not going to work. Their plan was to grab Enzio Bassalino's three sons by the balls sexually and mentally, destroying their lives, and by doing so reduce the old man to a wreck.

Bullshit.

No chance.

Still, Dukey decided he would let them play around until he was ready to put his own plan into action.

Things were getting involved, but he knew it was going to be *his* way in the end.

Rio paced around the apartment. "Dukey's going to be trouble," she warned.

"He always has been," Cass said dryly. "Why should now be any different?"

"I can't imagine him and Margaret together," Lara joined in.

"Oh, they were something together," Rio said. "Pure electricity. You know Margaret and her men. If they were easy, they bored her."

No, Lara wanted to say. I didn't know Margaret and her men. I wish I had. The truth was, she hadn't really known anything about Margaret's personal life, because she was always too busy talking about herself.

She glanced over at Beth, the other sister she didn't know at all. Silently she vowed to make up for the past. She wanted to get to know Beth properly.

"Well." Rio stood up. "I gotta make tracks. Four starving kids are waitin' for mama's presence."

"How old are your children?" Beth asked.

"Old enough to drive me *crazeee!*"

Cass stood up, too. The meeting was over. The decision was made.

Soon revenge would be theirs.

Chapter 8

Tall and good-looking, Nick Bassalino was the perfect Italian-American boy. Fine white teeth, often exposed in a ready smile, warm brown eyes, and longish black hair, slightly curling. He was thirty-three and favored black Italian suits, silk shirts, handmade shoes. Nothing but the best for Nick Bassalino.

He lived in style in a large house high above the lights of Hollywood. Not an actor, he'd had many offers because of his almost unbelievable good looks. It was only on close scrutiny that you might suspect his nose was fixed—it wasn't. His teeth capped—they weren't. And his jet-black hair slightly helped along by a bottle of dye—it wasn't.

Nick headed an import/export company called Warehousing Incorporated. It was the biggest outfit of its kind on the West Coast, and Nick was the boss.

When your father was Enzio Bassalino you certainly didn't start at the bottom.

Nick's current lady friend was April Crawford, an aging movie star with four husbands behind her. The starlets and dingalings were not for Nick. He liked to command a little respect when he went out, and in Hollywood the surest way of doing that was to be seen with a star.

They had been together a year. The arrangement suited both their public images. It pleased April that Nick had his own money and didn't freeload off her. He looked good, wasn't too young—not a baby—nothing to make a laughingstock of her. He got along with her friends, and of course—most important, as far as April was concerned—he was sensational in bed. Pure stud all the way.

As for Nick, he enjoyed the respectability of being with April, mixing with the movie colony, and seeing his picture in the fan magazines. April brought a little class into his life.

The one thing he didn't understand was why Enzio objected to the relationship so strongly. His father was always phoning him and complaining. "What's with you and the old bag? What's goin' on, Nick? You're making the name Bassalino a joke."

"Better I should be with a piece of beautiful, dumb eighteen-year-old cooze, I suppose," Nick would reply dourly.

"Yeah. Why not? Is it so terrible to have a pretty face, firm tits, a piece other men want—but you've got? Huh?"

"You just don't know," Nick would say, tired of the same old argument.

"So I don't know, big fuckin' deal. Only I haven't done too bad for an old man who don't know. An' *you* haven't done too bad by being my son."

"All right, all right. Forget it. I'll send you a telegram when we break up. You can go out an' celebrate."

"Schmuck!" Enzio would mutter, and they both ended up laughing. It was a weekly conversation.

The two of them had a relationship based on love, the fierce, proud love that binds an Italian family.

Whatever Enzio had done in his life—and he'd done plenty—he knew he had always been a good father to his boys. In spite of their mother's ill health (he always referred to Rose's madness as ill health), he'd brought them up to be fine men. Nick was doing a good job of running Warehousing Incorporated. He was tough; people thought twice about messing with him. Yes, Nick was a true son of Enzio Bassalino.

"Are you ready yet, darling?" April Crawford approached Nick in his dressing room. They had separate houses, but on weekends April liked him to stay with her.

April Crawford was a well-preserved blonde in her early fifties. She was petite, slim, perfectly groomed and made up. From a distance she looked late thirties, but up close tired little lines and a faint puffiness gave her secrets away.

"I'm always ready for you, sugar," Nick said cheerfully, grabbing her, making her squeal with pleasure.

He had been eight years old when he'd seen her on the screen for the first time and fallen in love.

"I think we should arrive early tonight," April said. After four husbands and numerous lovers she had never experienced such delights as Nick Bassalino had to offer.

"You're the boss."

"I wish we didn't have to go at all. Perhaps if I phoned Janine she'd understand. . . ."

"She will *not* understand," he said firmly. "We're gonna go. We're both dressed, and you look great—like a little doll." He had no intention of missing Janine Jameson's party. She was a contemporary of April's, and equally famous.

They rode to the party in Nick's black Mercedes. April wore a pale blue sequin dress. Some of the sequins came off and stuck to his clothes. He picked them off impatiently.

"Don't lean on me in that dress," he warned. He always liked to look immaculate.

"You're so fussy." She laughed gaily. "But I love you all the same."

At the party there were plenty of familiar faces—stars, directors, producers. Nick basked in the company. He loved show business.

A busty starlet approached him at the bar as he was ordering April a drink. They had made out once or twice, long before he met April.

"How's it going, Nicky Ticky?" the girl asked, thrusting her well-developed bosom toward him. "Getting fed up with grandma yet? 'Cos you know, any time you do, I'll be glad to hear from you."

"Hey, babe, what you gonna do when your tits drop?" he asked with a not-so-cavalier wink. "Better stop hustling an' take yourself a typing course, 'cause it don't look to me like it's gonna be too long."

"Cocksucker!" the girl muttered, furious.

"Excuse me, I have a *lady* waiting," Nick said amiably.

April didn't carry her liquor well. After two Scotches her speech started to slur, and shortly after that her walk became lopsided and her face went slack. In short, she fell to pieces.

It irritated Nick. He didn't drink much himself; in his business it paid to be alert, so he usually stuck to plain club soda. He was always warning April to cut her intake. That's why he tried to mix her drinks himself, carefully watering them down. But she was onto him and usually grabbed a fresh drink from every passing waiter.

Janine Jameson's party was no exception, and April was soon rolling in the aisles. Nick knew from past experience to keep his distance. Drunk, April became belligerent and insulting. A real pain in the ass.

He was talking to a lady gossip writer when he first saw the girl. She was standing by the bar with a group of people. She was of medium height, with golden-tanned skin and a mane of sun-streaked auburn hair. She had an exquisite body clad in a clinging long white dress, slit high. She was about the most spectacular-looking woman he'd ever seen—and in his time he'd seen a few.

"Who is *that*?" he couldn't help asking.

The lady gossip writer smiled. A crisp, bitchy smile. "Better not let April hear the hard-on in your voice," she warned. "The lady is Lara Crichton, one of those poor little rich girls whose picture is always in the fashion magazines."

He quickly changed the subject.

Lara spotted him immediately. After all, she had pictures of him, a short dossier on his life, and she knew all about his relationship with April Crawford.

After observing him across the room she angled herself at the bar so that when he glanced up she was directly in his line of vision.

When he first spotted her he did a classic double take.

First part—easy, but then the initial impact had always been easy for Lara. Ever since she could remember men had noticed her. Even when she was a small girl of seven and had been sent to London she had attracted attention. Very pretty, she'd had no trouble charming the childless couple she was staying with.

They worshiped her, and although they didn't have much money, they lavished everything they could on her.

Lara soon grew used to attention, and as she developed and grew she certainly received more than her fair share.

At fourteen she left school to study dancing, diction and movement. She entered a charm competition in a magazine and won. The price was a free modeling course at a reputable school where she was discovered by the best model agent in London, and shortly thereafter she became a successful teen model.

Photographers loved her; she had a chameleon quality essential for a good model. With no trouble at all she could look girlish, sophisticated, sexy, even plain. It was a matter of expression, and Lara mastered the art.

Her work was the most important part of her life. She dieted, exercised, ate health foods, and slept at least eight hours every night. Dates were unimportant, work was all-consuming.

Soon her incredible beauty deepened and bloomed, and she began to add polish to the diamond. She started to go out with specially selected men. One who could teach her about wine, another about racing, and yet another about baccarat, *chemin de fer*, and "twenty one."

She refused to sleep with any of them, although they all tried. She hadn't found the man to teach her about sex.

A week after her twentieth birthday she met Jamie P. Crichton and knew at once that this was the man she was destined to marry. Jamie had already inherited a trust fund worth several million pounds, and there was plenty more to come. He was young, good-looking, and arrogant. He was also surrounded by girls, and although his initial reaction to her was predictable, she knew that if she wasn't very careful, she could sink without a trace into the sea of females around him.

So she played it very smart, refusing to go out with him at all. Instead she cultivated his friends. Everywhere Jamie went, she was bound to be.

His best friend, Eddie Stephen Keys, fell madly in love with her and proposed. Lara wasn't prepared to settle for anything less than her original choice.

It took several months for her to get through to Jamie. And then suddenly one day he knew, and that was that. He chartered a jet, they got married in Tahiti, and the world press embraced them as the latest Beautiful Couple.

Their marriage lasted exactly one year. A year during which Lara became a celebrity.

Then just as suddenly it was over; they both wanted a divorce. They were equally bored by the restrictions of marriage and the drudgery of being with each other all the time.

It was a friendly parting of the ways. Jamie agreed to pay her a generous settlement, and she took off for Tijuana, where she got a quick divorce, and then on to Acapulco, where she met her first Italian prince.

Since that time Lara had moved around. All the best places at the best times with the best men. It was only when Margaret was shot that she finally stopped to think. What was she doing with her life? Why was it so important to be in the right place at the right time with the right man? Why did she constantly seek out hedonistic, boring escorts who could offer her nothing but money? Was it *that* exciting to be photographed at every airport? Quoted in every empty fashion magazine?

And why did she need to travel down the Nile? Safari in Africa? Ski in Gstaad? And summer in Sardinia?

On reflection, it all seemed such an empty life. The death of Margaret, traveling to New York, and spending time with Margaret's friends and her sister Beth had finally made her realize this.

Now her mind was made up. She was determined to help avenge Margaret's death.

Nick Bassalino was the perfect opportunity. And soon he would be all hers.

Lara had been brought to the party by Jeanette and Leslie Larson, a young couple whose only claim to fame was that Les's mother was one of the richest women in the world. Lara had arrived in L.A. several days before. She was staying with the Larsons as their houseguest, and they were thrilled to have her. Within a week she knew she'd get to meet Nick Bassalino, for April Crawford was known to be an avid partygoer. Running into him so soon was pure luck.

She pointed him out to Jeanette. "Who's that man?" she asked casually.

"I guess you mean Nick," Jeanette replied with a knowing laugh. "He's April Crawford's boyfriend, and he's *strictly* not up for grabs.

The guy is crazy about her, follows her around like a nanny. Why? Do you think he's attractive?"

"Is he an actor?" Lara asked, countering the question.

"No, he's some sort of hustler, wheeler-dealer. Les says he's a hood." Jeanette giggled. "You *do* find him attractive, don't you?"

"Not really." She faked a yawn. "A bit too obvious. All tight trousers and teeth."

Jeanette nodded. "Anyway, as I said, he's well taken care of, and let's face it, darling, hardly your style."

Lara wondered exactly what Jeanette thought her style was.

The party was a bore, but Lara knew that somehow she had to meet Nick. Sammy Albert, an actor with the reputation of a super stud, was busily trying to persuade her to split and go to a club called The Discotheque. She'd told him no three times, but he was enamored and continued to follow her around, trying to get her to change her mind.

"Do you know April Crawford?" she asked at last. "I'd love to meet her."

"Do I know April! I've had her!" Sammy joked, taking her over and introducing her.

April's eyes were bloodshot, her lipstick smeared. "Hello, dear," she said icily. Competition was not her favorite thing.

Lara turned on the charm and flattered the movie star as she steered the conversation to a mutual friend who lived in Rome.

Suddenly Nick appeared. Deftly removing the too-full glass from April's hand, which was slopping on her dress, he replaced it with a half-full one.

"Do you know Nick Bassalino?" April asked, patting him fondly. "This is Lara—Lara . . ."

"Crichton," Lara said, gazing directly at him as she accepted his firm handshake with an equally warm pressure of her own. The man was too handsome for his own good.

He had brown eyes, friendly and open. "Glad to meet you," he said.

Want to bet? she thought.

"Why don't we go to The Discotheque?" Sammy asked yet again. "April? Nick? Maybe one of you can persuade Lara to come, too."

"Wonderful idea," April said gaily. "I feel like dancing, and Janine's parties—dear girl that she is—do get rather stuffy."

"Will you come?" Sammy asked Lara.

She nodded. "I'd better tell Les and Jeanette."

"How about that?" Sammy said, watching her walk away. "Is she something or *what*?"

April laughed. "Sammy darling, every time you meet a new girl it's always a grand love affair for about a minute and a half."

"Just give me a minute and a half with this one and I'll be happy forever!"

When Lara returned they left. She went with Sammy in his Maserati, while April and Nick followed in the Mercedes.

"I could easily lose them," Sammy said, placing an amorous hand on her knee. "We could go by my place and pick up some outasite grass. Huh? What do you say?"

Lara removed his hot hand. "I gave it up," she replied coolly.

Sammy was speechless. He received thousands of fan letters a week from girls merely wanting to touch him, and this one didn't even care to go with him to his house. It had been a long time between turndowns.

The Discotheque was crowded as usual, but a table was soon cleared for Sammy Albert and April Crawford. Movie stars always got premium treatment; it was one of the fringe benefits of being famous.

April ordered a double Scotch and immediately dragged Sammy onto the tightly packed dance floor.

"They're old friends," Nick said, feeling the need to explain. "Sammy got his first break in one of April's films."

Lara smiled. "It doesn't bother me if it doesn't bother you."

"Hell, I don't care. I like April to enjoy

herself, it does her good. She's a great little gal, got a lot of energy, a real tiger!"

Lara looked at him intently to see if he was putting her on, but he didn't appear to be. He was watching April on the dance floor, a proud smile on his face.

"You and Sammy must be about the same age," she remarked.

He knew what she was getting at. "I don't know." He shrugged. "Who cares about age? You know something? April's got more energy in her little finger than I have in my whole body."

April this, and April that. Nick Bassalino was not going to be quite as easy to crack as she'd imagined. She was used to men falling about—married, single, it made no difference. One of Lara's famous quotes—printed all over the world—was "Most men are easy lays." She had always found that if there was a man she wanted, he was to be had.

Not that there had been that many. There was the count; he had lasted two years. Then the film star, only a few short months. After him the German prince, a year. And then the English lord, a mere eighteen months. The Greek shipowner had lasted nearly a year. And finally Prince Alfredo Masserini. She had thought that perhaps Alfredo was the right one. He had the film star's looks, the Greek shipowner's money, the English lord's youth, and the count's charm. But in spite of it all he'd turned out to be a self-centered egoist. Like me, she thought, with a short, brittle laugh.

"What are you laughing at?" Nick asked curiously, trying to keep his eyes off her cleavage.

"Nothing that would amuse you." She shook her head in a languid, sexual fashion so that her long, thick hair swirled forward.

He glanced at her quickly. This woman was incredibly beautiful. But what was beauty in a town like Hollywood? So many girls, so many different shades of sexy, pretty, and gorgeous. So many different shapes and sizes. Something to appeal to everyone. In Hollywood beauty was a commodity, a close relation of the hard sell.

April Crawford was something else. April was class, and distinction, and acceptance. April was a ticket to ride up there among all the movie idols he'd worshiped since he was a little kid.

Oh, no, he wasn't going to blow April out for a quick dip in this one's honey pot. April was a jealous lady, sharp, and full of pride. If she ever caught him straying, the shit would really hit in no uncertain fashion.

"I hope you're coming to the party Jeanette and Les are throwing for me tomorrow night," Lara said casually.

"April makes all our social arrangements. If

she knows about it, we'll be there. My lady hates missing a party."

Lara smiled and widened her eyes. "Great," she murmured.

What a schmuck this guy was—he was going to be easy.

Chapter 9

Frank Bassalino was Enzio's oldest son, and Enzio depended more on him than on the others, for when he had opted for semiretirement it was Frank who took over some of his more important business enterprises.

"One day," Enzio was proud of saying, "Frank is going to be The Man. One day not so far off."

Frank got along well with Enzio's older business associates. They were difficult men, quick to criticize, but he was managing to create a connection.

In some ways Frank was stronger than Enzio. Born and brought up in one of the tougher districts of New York, he'd always had to fight for what he wanted, in spite of his father's position.

Frank was not a man to cross. Thirty-six years old, he had worked for Enzio since he was sixteen and seen all aspects of his business. He had been involved in protection, prostitutes, dope, the numbers racket, hoisting. Once he had enjoyed being the hit man, but Enzio didn't approve. It was too risky and dangerous.

In his time Frank had been a womanizer in the true Bassalino tradition, going through an incredible number of females—used and thrown away like so many old Kleenex. Until, at the age of twenty-nine, he had seen a picture of Anna Maria, his cousin in Sicily, and immediately sent for her. She was fourteen years old and spoke no English. Enzio paid her family a dowry and arranged everything. When she arrived in America, Frank married her.

Like father like son. Both men had opted for a partner from the old country. Although unlike Rose, Anna Maria was timid and quiet. At twenty-one she still didn't speak much English.

Frank and Anna Maria lived in an old brownstone house in Queens with their four children, and she was expecting another.

Frank didn't stray much now. The occasional

hooker he could beat up was about his only weakness.

When the time came to put the revenge plan into action, Rio said she wanted a shot at Frank Bassalino. She was outvoted. According to the extensive dossier they'd managed to get on him, she wasn't his scene, not his style at all. No, they all decided, the only chance with a man like Frank Bassalino was someone fresh and innocent. A girl who would remind him of his wife when he'd first brought her to America. Beth was the obvious choice.

It turned out that there was a perfect opportunity. Frank was looking for a nanny to teach his children English. He had registered with three employment agencies and turned down all the applicants, who were mostly black or Mexican. It was decided Beth should apply for the job.

She changed her hippie clothes and put on a plain blouse and skirt. Then, with her pale hair tied back, her simple outfit, and her false references, she turned up at his house for an interview.

A maid showed her into an old-fashioned living room. The furniture was worn, and there were many religious pictures on the walls. Beth glanced around, her heart racing with anticipation.

She waited for over half an hour, and then

Frank Bassalino strode into the room with Anna Maria hovering behind him.

He was a powerful-looking man with black hair, hooded dark eyes, a moody mouth, and a beaky nose. He was attractive in a brutal way.

Beth loathed him on sight. She knew men like him—big, violent men who resented any change. Men whose physical strength was their prime weapon.

With an involuntary shudder she remembered the night at the commune when men like Frank Bassalino had come calling in the middle of the night. There were eight or nine of them, and they were drunk.

The band of drunken louts had roared up in two cars, laughing and swigging from bottles of booze. The farm was situated well off the main road. There were no neighbors, no one to whom they could run for help.

The front door wasn't locked, and the men had burst drunkenly in, kicking the old sheepdog, Shep, until he was a beaten pulp. Then they had dragged the girls out of bed and raped them one by one while the boys were roughed up, laughingly, methodically. The men had jeered and called them names, told them to get a haircut and a job and stop piss-assing around.

It was no match. The men were big and strong and filled with the righteous power of do-gooders.

"If you were my daughter," one of them had

hissed in Beth's ear as he'd pumped away inside her, "I'd tan your hide until you couldn't walk for a week."

Before leaving they'd cut the boys' hair, crudely hacking away with a rusty pair of kitchen scissors. Max had needed seventeen stitches in his scalp.

This outrage had taken place two years before, yet Beth still slept unsoundly, still felt revulsion when faced with a man like Frank.

"Hmmm." He looked her over. "You're kinda young, huh?"

"I'm twenty," she replied. "I've been working with children for the past three years. Did you read my references?"

He was surprised to see such a young and pretty girl. It was almost too good to be true after some of the garbage the agency had sent him. His kids would love this one, she looked so clean and nice.

There was no point in playing games. "Listen, you want the job—it's yours. You get your own room, decent food, and a coupla nights off a week. Okay?"

She nodded. Was it all going to be as easy as this? "Can I see the children?" she asked.

"Sure. Hey—Anna Maria." He pulled his wife forward, a shy, dark girl with puffy features and a huge belly. "You take—uh—what's your name again?"

"Beth."

"Yeah, yeah. Beth, meet Mrs. Bassalino—my wife. She don't talk much English—maybe you can teach her, too. She'll take you to see the kids, show you around. Any problems, you come to me. Just remember, I'm a busy man, so make sure there ain't too many problems. Got it? When can you start?"

Her heart was pounding. "Tomorrow," she said, hiding her excitement.

"Good girl. Anna Maria's about to pop any time now. Some help around here is just what we need."

He gave Anna Maria a shove in her direction, looked Beth over one more time, and left.

Chapter 10

Angelo Bassalino had been sent to London after the trouble. It was only a temporary move, a discreet way of getting rid of him until the Camparo family calmed down. Gina Camparo was to be married soon, and after the ceremony—a few months, perhaps—the whole incident would be forgotten, and Angelo could be brought safely home.

Enzio had been somewhat amused by the whole affair. Angelo was his true son, a boy who let nothing stand in the way of his fine upstanding Bassalino prick.

But it had been a touchy situation, and if

Angelo had not been Enzio's son, he might have found himself lodging inside a block of cement at the bottom of the East River. To screw a girl was one thing, but not at her engagement party to another man, and not where her brother and fiancé could discover you. And not when the girl was the daughter of a powerful rival—albeit a friendly one.

So Angelo was dispatched to London. There were gambling interests he could take care of there, and without too much effort Enzio arranged everything.

Angelo was not up to his expectations businesswise. The boy had none of the Bassalino drive or ambition. He had no hard core of toughness to call upon when dealing with people.

Enzio reasoned that Angelo was only twenty-four, a baby; he had plenty of time to wise up. But he also remembered himself at twenty-four, a veteran of six successful hits, already Crazy Marco's right-hand man, a man with a big future ahead of him.

In New York, Angelo had worked for Frank.

"He's a lazy little punk," Frank constantly complained. "You send him to a joint to shake loose some tight cash, and you hafta send another guy chasing *him* 'cos he's shacked up with some broad. Cooze, that's all he's got on his mind."

Enzio tried sending him out to the coast to

work for Nick, but that was even worse. Angelo fell for a sexy starlet and ended up getting his ass beaten off by her "producer."

"You'd better get yourself together in London," Enzio warned him. "A Bassalino should command respect. Screw around all you want, but you gotta remember—*work* is the important thing—an' *money*. There's solid opportunities for setting up over there, an' one of these days I wanna see you control our end of it. To begin with, you work with the Stevesto organization—they'll show you around."

Angelo had shrugged. He didn't care about making money—as long as there was plenty in the family, why did he have to work his butt off scoring more? It didn't make sense. Let Frank and Nick keep the Bassalino respect going—they enjoyed it, he didn't.

But he didn't argue with his father. Nobody argued with Enzio. There had been a time when he had expressed a wish not to go into the family "business." He'd wanted to be an actor, or maybe a musician. At sixteen those were his ambitions. When Enzio found out about it he'd beaten him with a leather strap and locked him in his room for a week. Angelo never mentioned it again.

London was a fine town, as Angelo soon discovered. Lots of pretty girls and friendly people. A person could walk the streets without fear of getting beaten up and robbed.

An apartment had been arranged for him, and he went to work for the Stevesto setup. It was easy potatoes; all he had to do was keep his eye on a couple of casinos and begin getting the hang of things.

Angelo was happy. He could have a different girl every week if he felt like it, and he did feel like it. He had to have sex every day. It was a habit—like morning coffee or doing push-ups—a habit he enjoyed excelling at.

Angelo was not tall and muscular like his brothers. He was slighter in build, almost skinny. And his face was more angular, with high cheekbones. He liked to wear his hair thick and long—a minor freak-out—and sometimes he featured a Che mustache and stubbly beard.

"You look like a fuckin' commie," Enzio was always screaming at him. "Jesus! Whyn't you cut off that hair, buy some decent clothes—a suit maybe. You look like shit. Why can't you take after your brothers?"

Fuck his brothers. Angelo kept his personal appearance exactly as he wanted. It was about the only way he could spit in his father's eye without doing too much damage.

The full contingent of English press turned out at Heathrow Airport to meet Rio Java. Her reputation always preceded her.

She stepped off the plane in an outlandish

pink catsuit, trailing a full-length leopard-skin coat over one arm.

"Hi, boys," she greeted the army of photographers. "What do you want me to do?"

What *didn't* they want her to do. Rio Java was always good for a front-page picture.

She had been making headlines for years. A heroin addict at eighteen, Rio had first been discovered in a rehab center by the very famous avant-garde film maker, Billy Express, who was making a movie about drugs called *Turn On/ Turn Off*. His intrusive camera followed her every move as she was given the treatment—the cure. He didn't miss a thing, and the result was instant stardom. It wasn't long before she moved into his life permanently, gave birth to his baby (an event he filmed in loving if somewhat lurid detail), and starred in all his future projects. Billy Express was extremely successful and very, very rich. The more pornographic of his movies had made him a fortune.

Rio lived with Billy and his entourage in an elegant New York brownstone he shared with his mother. It was not the ideal arrangement, but his mother—a former Ziegfeld girl—came with the package.

Rio felt she owed Billy a lot. He was responsible for making her a celebrity, and she loved every minute of her notoriety. Off heroin, she had no objections to joining Billy, his friends, *and* his mother on their constant LSD trips. One memorable night she found herself sharing Billy's bed with his Chinese boyfriend, Lei. It amused Billy to have them make it together while he filmed their lovemaking. The result was that Rio became pregnant again, and Billy was delighted. He loved children and lost no time in having the top floor of his house redecorated as a nursery, just in time for the birth of Rio's twins—two tiny Chinese boys.

They were all happy. Billy, his bizarre mother, Lei, the children, the entourage. They made their movies, threw outrageous parties, and existed in a sort of delicious, stoned vacuum.

Until one day Rio met Larry Bolding. He was a very straight married senator in his mid-forties. He came to one of Billy's parties, and Rio took one look at the suntanned face, the suit, the honest eyes, and flipped out. There was something about Larry Bolding that attracted her with a passion.

"I *have* to have him," she whispered to Billy.

"No problem," he replied easily—jealousy was an emotion unknown to Billy. He selected a pill from his pocket. "Slip this in his drink and he's all yours."

In a rare moment of clarity Rio decided against spiking the senator's drink. She wanted him without having to resort to drugs. She wanted *him* to want *her*.

Larry Bolding had a politician's smile and a very direct gaze. Rio went to work. She was no slouch when it came to seduction.

It took some time to get him to a bedroom. More time to get him undressed. He was so sweet! He actually wore patterned Jockey shorts and an undershirt.

Rio launched into her specialties. He was more interested in straight screwing.

It was the start of a six-month affair. An affair that had to be kept secret, due to the fact he was a married man.

Rio understood. He gave her the age-old story about how he and his wife just stayed together for appearances, and worldly as she was, she believed him.

After a few weeks she told Billy she couldn't sleep with him anymore. In fact, because Larry didn't approve of her setup, she moved out and took an apartment in the Village. It was more convenient for Larry, more private.

Billy gave her a generous allowance and kept the children with him, because they both agreed it was for the best. She visited them every other day.

Eventually Billy decided he wanted her to do a new movie he'd written. After all, she was his superstar.

Larry Bolding said he didn't want her to do it. He preferred to keep her always available, as he never knew when he could see her.

"The guy is an asshole," Billy warned. "He's going to ruin you."

But Rio was in love and didn't listen. Instead she turned very straight for Larry, doing everything he told her to. She gave up drugs, drinking, parties; no screwing (except for him), no outlandish makeup, and no weird clothes.

Larry's visits grew fewer and fewer. Eventually they stopped altogether.

Rio was destroyed. In vain she tried to contact him, but the barriers were up. There was no way of getting past the many secretaries and aides. Absolutely no way of letting him know she was pregnant with his child.

When she finally realized she'd been used, it hurt more than she ever thought possible. One gloomy Saturday night she slashed her wrists and fortunately was found by a neighbor. The neighbor turned out to be Margaret Lawrence Brown.

It took Rio a long time to get over the way Larry Bolding had treated her. She developed a deep resentment of the way women allowed themselves to be used by men. Especially married men.

She listened to Margaret, and her words made sense. Why waste time brooding about the past when the future was all that really mattered?

Without his ever knowing, she gave birth to Larry Bolding's baby—a little girl. Billy Express suggested she move back in with him and her other children. It wasn't the way she wanted to live anymore, and she told him. She also told him she wanted her children to come and live with her. Billy said no, they would stay with him.

This clash of wills resulted in a long-drawn-out court battle that Rio finally won. She got her children back in spite of the abuse Billy Express publicly hurled at her. He was enraged.

They all stood up in the witness box and testified about what a bad mother she was, every one of her so-called friends, the entourage, and Billy's mother.

Margaret Lawrence Brown testified on her behalf, and in the end she got her children.

It was a juicy court case. The newspapers and gossips loved every minute of it.

Afterward, Rio was inundated with film scripts. Everyone had a project she would be perfect for.

Soon she started to work again and never looked back.

Now she was in London, and she was there for one purpose only.

Angelo Bassalino and the revenge.

She would destroy him as only she knew how.

Chapter 11

Old friends though they were, Bosco Sam wanted his money back, with interest, and Dukey K. Williams just didn't have it.

Dukey was hanging around in New York, still living in the apartment he had shared with Margaret, brooding about her murder.

"Come on, man, you gotta get back in action," his manager pleaded daily.

"Cancel everything," Dukey told him. "I'm gonna sit still awhile an' get my head straight." Margaret's murder had left a deep void in his life. He couldn't come to terms with her death.

He canceled all his work dates, a European tour, and a recording session for a new album. Several promoters threatened lawsuits.

Dukey didn't care. "Fuck 'em" was his only comment. He was not making any money, and the royalties coming in from record sales were going straight into the pocket of ex-wife number one and two "ex-children." He called them ex-children because his wife—the redheaded bitch—had obtained a court order forbidding him to see them.

Bosco Sam was not prepared to give up. "I want my money," he said, his tone becoming more threatening as each day passed. "If it was anyone but you, Dukey . . ."

They had struggled through school together, known each other a long time.

"Let's meet," Dukey suggested, thinking fast. "Maybe we can cut a deal."

"Yeah, let's do that." An ominous pause. "While you're still alive."

They met at the zoo. Bosco Sam had a thing about privacy; he made sure that all his important meetings took place in public venues.

"I'll probably get mobbed," Dukey complained. But it was a crisp October morning, and the Central Park zoo was almost deserted.

They were hardly an inconspicuous pair—Dukey in his calf-length, belted mink trench coat, boots, and huge shades, and Bosco Sam, a camel-hair-coated, three-hundred-pound man with an attitude problem.

"Fuckin' park," Bosco Sam complained. "Only place a deal can get it on anymore."

"Here's the action," Dukey said as they strolled in front of the monkeys. "Word's on the street you're about ready to dance with the Crowns. You and them make sweet soul music while Frank Bassalino gets the short ones plucked. Beautiful. No sweat. But how would it grab you if *I* did the plucking? Frank, the brothers, Enzio. The whole Bassalino bag of shit."

"You?" Bosco Sam said, starting to laugh. "Jesus! You sound like an elephant farting!"

Bosco Sam heaved with even more laughter.

"Listen, man," Dukey continued. "I ain't layin' no shit on you, you hear me talkin'? I'm serious. For the two hundred thou—you're out of it. Your hands are clean. There'll be no heat knockin' on *your* door. Nobody's gonna know 'bout our little deal 'cept you an' me. Am I reachin' you, bro?"

"Yeah," said Bosco Sam thoughtfully. "Yeah . . ."

"It'll be cool. Keep up the pressure till it blows. An' you with a powdered fuckin' ass nobody can suspect."

Bosco Sam started to laugh. "You still cut it. Big fuckin' star, but you still foxy as Puerto Rican tail!"

"Hey—I'll throw in a song or two at your daughter's wedding."

"The kid's only ten."

"So I'll be around when I'm needed. How about it? We all set to jive or what?"

"Yeah, I'll give you a shot at it. Why the fuck not? We go back a long way. Just remember—you give me results or no deal. Understood?"

"Right on."

"Who you gonna use?"

"I got my own ideas."

Bosco Sam spat on the ground. "If you're smart you'll use Leroy Jesus Bauls. He'll cost you, but that black motherfucker don't know no fear—that's why we call him Black Balls!"

One of the monkeys let out a loud screech.

"Shit!" exclaimed Bosco Sam. "That fuckin' monkey just pissed all over me!"

"It's lucky," Dukey said, managing to keep a straight face.

"It better be," Bosco Sam grumbled. "Or your bones gonna be *dead* fuckin' bones."

Chapter 12

Lara's effect on Nick was slow but lethal.

They met again at the party Jeanette and Les threw for her, and then again at a screening of a new Dustin Hoffman film.

Lara was seeing Sammy Albert, fighting him off, because to get involved with him sexually was a diversion she did not need. It was at her suggestion that Sammy invited April and Nick to dinner at the Bistro.

Confident that this was the night, Sammy was in a buoyant mood.

Lara put on her Yves Saint Laurent black-velvet jacket, cut man's style, and underneath it a high-necked blouse in black chiffon which, when you looked closely, was see-through. Underneath she wore no bra, and the effect was incredibly sexy because as she moved the jacket moved, too, exposing her and then falling back into place.

"Now you see them, now you don't," Sammy announced proudly at the beginning of the evening.

Nick and April started to fight halfway through dinner, a whispered argument no one was supposed to hear, because above all April would never blow her image by showing a jealous streak.

The champagne Sammy had insisted on was beginning to have its effect. "For God's sake, get your eyes off her bloody tits!" April hissed angrily at Nick.

Nick, who had been making a concerted effort *not* to look, was insulted. "Cool down, April," he muttered. "Don't make a fool of yourself."

"Cool down," she mimicked. "Just *who* do you think you're talking to, little man?"

"I'm talking to you, and goddamn it—you've had enough." He gripped her wrist as she lifted her glass.

Furious, she tried to shake free, and the champagne spilled down the front of her dress.

"Oh, dear." Lara was the first there with a napkin, dabbing it dry. "I don't think it will stain."

"It's only an old rag," April said, recovering her composure and shooing Lara away. "Nick, dear, you're *so* clumsy." She turned her back on both of them and began to talk to Sammy on her other side.

Lara glanced at Nick and smiled sympathetically. He grinned back, allowing his eyes to drop briefly to her breasts. If he was going to get accused, he might as well do it.

She was still looking at him, her green eyes probing and interested.

He felt a sudden uncomfortable tightness in his pants, a feeling he had long ago learned to control. Christ, this girl was really something—she was getting to him in no uncertain way. In the year he had been with April he'd only taken chances twice. Once, on a business trip to Vegas, a faceless showgirl with incredible legs. The other, a redhead he'd met at the beach on one of his rare afternoons off. Neither of the girls had known who he was or anything about him. That way there was no risk of April ever finding out.

"Let's go to The Discotheque," Sammy was saying.

"Yes, marvelous idea," April agreed, downing another glass of champagne.

Nick didn't try to stop her. Tonight it was her problem, let her get good and boozed up. She would be sorry in the morning.

There was more champagne at The Discotheque, and Lara noticed that even Nick was drinking, something she had never seen him do before.

She danced with Sammy and was embarrassed by his convulsive, almost obscene way of moving. One thing about European men, Prince Alfredo especially—they knew how to keep their cool on the dance floor. Sammy hopped about like a baby elephant jerking off.

When she sat down April invited her to accompany her to the ladies' room. She went, because half the initial battle was remaining friendly with the aging movie star.

"I think you're right, darling," April observed, studying herself in the mirror. "Look at my dress—all dry and not a stain in sight." She produced a lethal tube of scarlet lipstick from her purse and jammed it on, going above and below her natural lip line as a series of studio makeup artists had taught her to do.

They stood side by side, observing themselves in the full-length mirror. April could easily have been Lara's mother, but she didn't realize this. As far as she was concerned, her reflection was just as smooth and youthful as that of the girl beside her.

"Isn't Sammy a darling boy?" she commented. "Such fun. I do hope you realize how lucky you are."

"Lucky?" Lara questioned, brushing her hair.

"Well, of course, darling. Sammy's *very* much in demand, and I can see he's absolutely crazy about you."

Lara smiled slightly, sensing what was coming next.

"Real men are few and far between in this town." April hiccupped elegantly. "I should know, I married four of them." More lipstick. "Now take Nick, for instance. He's good-looking enough, but what does he have to offer, darling? There's more to it than just being a good fuck. Confidentially, I need a little more from a man, you know what I mean?"

Lara nodded. "Yes, I know what you mean." She knew exactly what April meant—stick with Sammy and keep your hands off my Nick. He's taken.

Leaning forward, April examined her teeth closely in the mirror, removing any telltale lipstick stains. "I adore your blouse, darling, you must tell me where you bought it. Of course, Nick's not a man for boobs, he's a leg man." April hoisted her skirt, exposing still-perfect legs. "Although I doubt very much if he'd allow me to wear a top like that. He's really very prudish. It's the Italian side of him, you know." She stepped back, liked what she saw, and added, "Ah, well, back to the champagne."

Lara lingered in the ladies' room. April didn't have to tell *her* about Italians; the only time they were prudish was if you were their wife.

She wondered if Nick wanted to marry April. The woman was still good-looking for her age, and of course there was the fame thing. April Crawford was a name that had once been right up there with Lana Turner, Ava Gardner, and the other famous Crawford. That had to be the attraction.

Lara sighed. She knew quite a bit about Nick, but there was still plenty to find out.

By the time she returned to their table April was dancing with Sammy, while Nick sat alone.

"Hi." Sliding into her seat, she shrugged off her jacket, allowing him the full view.

He looked. He couldn't help himself.

"It's hot, isn't it?" she said, although there was no reason to make an excuse.

"Very."

They locked stares, holding the look for several beats too long.

"Would you like to dance?" he asked.

"Yes."

They got up, and he took her by the arm, steering her to the small, tightly packed dance floor. The Stones were at full shout.

Facing each other, they went through the

ritualistic moves. He was a good dancer, tight, controlled, and at ease. The sounds were too loud for talk. Across the floor Sammy Albert and April Crawford made fools of themselves. Suddenly the music changed, and Isaac Hayes was singing "Never Can Say Good-bye." It was slow, throbbing, and sensual.

Nick stared at her again, his brown eyes intent and moody. He pulled her slowly toward him, his nails digging into her flesh under the black chiffon.

Lara shivered slightly; this man was dangerously good-looking. When she was close to him she felt the proof of his attraction, and for one short moment the music, the feel of his maleness, it all combined to make her want to forget everything and just be with him. Surrendering to the feeling, she pressed close against him.

"Hey, baby, I don't have to tell you how I feel," he muttered. "No—I don't have to tell you—you know—you knew from the first time we saw each other."

Managing to push him away a little, she shook her head.

"I've got to see you," he said urgently. "How about lunch tomorrow? We could meet at the beach, somewhere quiet where no one would see us."

"Wait a minute." She took a deep breath, pushing him away completely. They stood in the midst of the swaying dancers. "*I* can see you any time," she said challengingly. *"I'm* not tied down."

He pulled her back into a tight embrace. "Listen, baby, you know my scene with April. She's a great lady. I wouldn't want to hurt her."

"Then don't," Lara replied crisply, back in control.

"Ah, come on," he said. "You feel the same way I do, I *know* you do. If I was to slide my hands under those tight pants of yours, I could prove it to you—you'd be—"

She cut him short, her green eyes wide and appealing. "Nick, I'm not arguing. Let's go home now. You say good-bye to April, and I'll kiss Sammy on the cheek. Then I'll take off my tight pants for you and—"

"Hey, you're beginning to sound like a bitch." He was angry.

Her eyes gleamed. "What's the matter? Don't you like it when I'm honest? If we both want each other so much, what's the big hang-up?"

"You *know* the hang-up," he groaned.

"Yes, I think I do, and I'll tell you something, Nick, it's all yours." She walked off the dance floor and rejoined April and Sammy at their table.

With a jolt she realized for a moment she'd almost lost control. What a stupid thing to do. Purely physical.

"Having fun?" April asked tensely.

Lara grabbed Sammy's arm. "Not nearly as much as I'm going to. Right, Sammy?"

He couldn't believe his luck. The ice queen was finally thawing. "You'd better believe it, honey. They don't call me action man for nothing!"

Chapter 13

The only time Beth saw Frank Bassalino was on Sundays. It appeared to be the only day he spent at home. Weekdays he was up and away before anyone was awake, returning late in the evenings after the household was asleep.

Sundays he spent with his children. In the morning he took them to the park, then home for a huge lunch of various pastas that Anna Maria spent the morning preparing. In the afternoon he played with them, absorbing himself in their interests. Cars and trains with the two boys, perhaps a game with his six-year-old daughter—his obvious favorite—and complicated building stacks with the two-year-old.

He was a good father, if you could call devoting one day a week to his children being a good father.

Anna Maria was a placid, almost stupid girl. She had no particular desire to learn English. Frank and the children conversed with her in Italian, and since they were her whole life, what was the point in learning to speak to other people? She spent her days baking, sewing, and writing letters to her family in Sicily. It was a rare day when she left the house.

Beth found the children to be well-behaved and easy to manage. She gave them an hour's coaching in English a day, and they seemed to enjoy it, even the little ones. There wasn't much else to do. The older children went to school, and the two-year-old slept in the afternoons.

After two weeks she met with Cass. "I don't think it's going to work," she said despairingly. "I never get to see him. And when I do he doesn't even notice me."

Cass had always thought Beth wasn't the type to be involved in the revenge. She agreed. "It's a crazy idea anyway. You should get out. We'll find someone else to take care of Frank."

Beth thought longingly of the commune, her own child, Chyna, and her boyfriend, Max. It was tempting to say yes to Cass, pack her things, and leave. But that would be admitting defeat, and she wanted to accomplish just as much as the others. She had to.

"I'm not quitting," she said firmly. "I'll get to him somehow. How are Lara and Rio making out?"

"Everything takes time," Cass replied evenly, wishing she had Margaret to turn to for advice. "I'm meeting with Dukey tonight. I'm sure he's going to agree with me about you. Honestly, Beth, you shouldn't be involved."

"Why not?" Beth's face flushed. "Don't forget I'm Margaret's sister. *I* want to do something just as much as the others. And I can—you'll see."

Cass sighed. "You aren't cut out for this. I said so from the beginning."

"Well, I'm involved now," Beth said stubbornly. "And I have no intention of stopping until the job is done."

That evening Beth waited. She put on a long white cotton nightdress, frilled and virginal. Then she brushed her straight blond hair loose. She looked very young and appealing.

The bedroom she occupied overlooked the front of the house, and she waited patiently by the window. At two in the morning a car drew up with three men inside. Frank and another man got out and walked over to the front door. Once Frank was inside his bodyguard returned to the car, and after a few moments it drove off. Frank was safely home.

Beth remained at the window, her mouth dry with anticipation. She knew Frank's routine so well. First he would go to his dressing room, where he would change into his pajamas and robe. Then into the big, old-fashioned kitchen, where he would make himself coffee and toast.

Another car moved slowly past the house. Its headlights dipped; two men were inside. Frank seemed to have bodyguards to look after the bodyguards.

Still she waited, not moving, shivering slightly. What if she went to the kitchen and he wanted her? What then? She didn't know how to maneuver people, pull the strings. She wasn't like Lara or Rio.

Frank Bassalino was a hard, strong man. How *did* one destroy a man like that?

Thoughts of Margaret drifted through her head. And of Enzio Bassalino—the man who'd ordered Margaret to be assassinated.

Beth knew she had to avenge her sister's death. And she knew exactly what had to be done.

Frank was brooding and thoughtful. There was trouble all over. The cops were tightening up, more money or further harassment. The Crown gang were causing disturbance; something would have to be done about those sons of bitches. On top of everything else, Enzio was driving him crazy, phoning to complain about this and that. The old man must have spies everywhere. Enzio Bassalino was supposed to be retired; why the fuck didn't he keep his nose out of business that wasn't his anymore?

There was also the protection problem. Several restaurants and clubs under the "security" of Frank Bassalino and his organization were being leaned on to put their faith in other directions. There had been a few unfortunate incidents, and the owners of certain establishments were beginning to wonder why they should pay protection to Frank Bassalino, *and* the cops, and *still* get hit.

Frank suspected a black group headed by narcotics king Bosco Sam was behind the trouble.

Rumor had it Bosco Sam had big plans for muscling in on Bassalino and Crown territories.

Frank had sent out word he was prepared to meet with Bosco Sam to discuss things.

In the meantime the clubs and restaurants were persuaded it was in their best interests to keep up their payments. It was a problem Frank was confident he could deal with on his own.

At home there was Anna Maria, with her belly so swollen a man couldn't even get a good fuck anymore, and Frank didn't like to go elsewhere. The last time had been bad. Esther's place, a new girl. Esther *knew* what he was like, so he figured the hooker would be prepared. She was a black-eyed girl, full-breasted and meaty-thighed. He'd turned her over and rammed it to her from behind. A slow count of ten, then wham—he'd pulled her head back and started to slap her, squeezing her breasts, hands paddling her buttocks.

As he got rougher the whore began to struggle and fight back. He enjoyed this action until she started to scream. Her nose was bleeding, and the whole thing was a mess. The bitch was yelling for the cops, and it took Esther some time to calm her down.

Frank left, angry and moody. It hadn't been satisfactory. That had been two weeks previously, and now he would have to make do with Anna Maria.

Ah, in the beginning his wife had been so sweet. Ripe and lovely. Young and untouched.

As he was thinking this, Beth entered the kitchen. She was like a dream come true.

"Excuse me, Mr. Bassalino," she said in a low voice. "I didn't realize anyone was up. I couldn't sleep and thought I would make some warm milk."

"Warm milk is for old maids," he said slowly. Christ! He'd never realized how delicate and pretty she was.

With a nervous laugh she took the milk carton from the fridge.

He watched her as she bent to take a pan from the cupboard and began to pour the milk into it. She wore no makeup. He liked that. Women who plastered on the gunk always reminded him of hookers. Hot, dirty tarts in black bras and garter belts. The kind his father liked. The kind his father had introduced him to when he was thirteen years of age.

"The job workin' out?" he asked.

"Yes, thank you, Mr. Bassalino." She concentrated on stirring the milk, a curtain of fine blond hair falling across her face.

"The kids treatin' you okay?"

"Yes, they're lovely children." She turned to look at him, and he got a whiff of virgin skin.

At that moment Beth knew everything was set. If only she could go through with it and hide her revulsion.

"Uh . . . you're a nice-looking girl," he said. "How come you're hidin' away watchin' someone else's kids?"

"I enjoy leading a quiet life, Mr. Bassalino."

"You do, huh?" He stared at her reflectively.

The milk began to boil. Beth watched it bubble and froth to the top of the pan until it finally cascaded over the top and onto her hand.

She screamed out in genuine pain.

"What the f—" Frank started to say. Then he saw what she'd done and smothered her hand in great globs of butter.

"I'm sorry." She stared at him with very blue vulnerable eyes. "I guess I wasn't concentrating on what I was doing."

They were close, so close that the very smell of him made her want to run. Instead she forced herself to lean even nearer.

Without warning he picked her up, holding her under the arms the way you lift a child, and commenced to kiss her—slowly at first, and then stronger, harder.

She didn't say anything, allowing her lips to stay dry and closed, puckering them only slightly.

"Christ!" he exclaimed. "You're so light, like one of the kids. Shit! You don't even know how to kiss. How old *are* you, anyway?"

She was a captive in his arms. He had such enormous strength she felt he could crush her to bits if he wanted to.

"I'm twenty," she whispered.

"Have you ever had a man?"

Valiantly she attempted to push away from him. "Mr. Bassalino—please—you're hurting me. Let go."

He released her abruptly. "You know what I want to do?" he said thickly. "You know what, honey?"

She nodded, lowering her eyes.

There was no stopping him now. "We'll go to your room," he said gruffly. "Nobody's gonna know. You ever done it before?"

He was hoping she would say no. He hadn't had a virgin since Anna Maria. In fact, the only other women he had been with had all been prostitutes.

"I'm not a virgin," she said, the rehearsed lines flowing easily. "Once before, when I was very young—only twelve—my stepfather came to my room. He was drunk. I didn't understand what he was doing. Later I had a baby. There's been no one since."

Frank digested this information silently. It appealed to him. One time with a drunken relative, it hardly counted. And only twelve at the time.

He slid his hand beneath the bodice of her nightgown.

"Mr. Bassalino, I can't." Her eyes were wide with fear. "Your wife, the children, it's not right . . ."

"I'll pay you," he said, watching her shrewdly. "One hundred dollars—cash. How about *that*?"

Shaking her head, she said, "I don't think you understand. I do find you attractive, but the circumstances are wrong. I'm employed by you. I have your trust and your wife's. If we—

well, you know—how could I face myself tomorrow?"

He was impressed with the girl's honesty. He didn't come across many people who had scruples; it made a refreshing change. However, it still didn't solve the problem of what he had for her. "How about if I fire you?" he suggested.

"That's a silly idea. Besides, I need the job."

He was fascinated by her soft blond hair, virgin hair. He had an urge to wrap it around his feet—other things. He wanted her now. Nobody got away with refusing Frank Bassalino.

"What do you want?" he asked thickly. Experience told him there was always a price.

"Nothing," she whispered. "I knew when I first saw you I shouldn't have taken the job. You're the first man I sensed was different. I knew you'd understand." She paused, playing him like a fish. "You're also the first man I've felt anything for." Her eyes were downcast. "But you're married. So it's impossible."

"Nothin's impossible," he said, wrapping her up in his big arms again, and smothering her with kisses while his hands roamed over her body.

She struggled—a futile act; he was even stronger than the men who'd raped her.

Exhaustion overcame her, and a feeling of relief. It would happen soon, it was what he wanted, and it was exactly what she had planned.

She hardly noticed him carrying her to her room. All the while he was mumbling, "It's gonna be all right. Nobody's gonna know."

She was glad she'd smoked a joint earlier; it had certainly taken the edge off things, made her as relaxed as she could be under the circumstances.

Roughly pulling off her nightgown, he locked the door and struggled out of his clothes.

"I'm not going to hurt you," he promised, crawling all over her. "It won't be like before. You'd better believe it."

Recoiling from the weight of his body, she shut her eyes as he pushed her legs apart. And then she felt him, and the tension slipped away, and she almost smiled.

Frank Bassalino was endowed with no greater gift than a ten-year-old boy.

Chapter 14

Leroy Jesus Bauls stood motionless at the door to the restaurant. His hard cinnamon eyes flicked slowly over the occupants, finally coming to rest on one man sitting at a corner table.

The maître d' was walking toward Leroy, his mouth open, ready to say there was no room. It was a fancy restaurant, and they didn't encourage blacks, even if they were well-dressed and expensive-looking, like Leroy.

But before the maître d' could reach him Leroy had placed the parcel he was carrying on the floor, given it a swift kick in the direction of the corner table, turned, and left.

The maître d' scratched his head in a puzzled fashion and started toward the parcel.

On television later that night there was a full report of the incident. The Magic Garden, a popular Manhattan restaurant, had been blown apart by a bomb. Fourteen people were dead, twenty-four injured. The police were working on several leads.

"Bull*shit*," muttered Leroy Jesus Bauls, walking over and switching the television off.

"What did you say, hon?" a black girl of startling beauty asked. She was in her mid-twenties, with curled auburn hair and almond-shaped brown eyes.

"Nothin'," Leroy replied. "Nothin' to interest you."

"Everything about you interests me," she whispered, nuzzling up behind him, stroking his hair.

Impatiently he shook her off. How nice it would be to find a girl able to keep her hands off him.

Leroy was twenty-two. Six feet, slight of build but extremely strong. Straight features, perfectly symmetric, inherited from his Swedish mother. Dark brown skin, inherited from his Jamaican father.

He was always dressed impeccably. Suits, vests, silk shirts. Even his socks and undershorts were made of the purest silk.

Leroy favored black as a color, in clothes, women, cars, and furniture.

His mother had given him the taste for expensive things. His mother had also turned him off white people for life.

"How about catching a movie tonight?" the girl asked. "We could go to the late show. I'm not working tomorrow, so—"

"I don't think so, Melanie," he said. "*I* have to work later."

"What do you do?" Melanie asked curiously. She had known him for three weeks, slept with him for two, and still knew nothing about him except that he had a nice apartment and plenty of money and was interesting to be with.

"I've told you, don't be nosy," Leroy said, his voice flat. "I do . . . uh . . . things that wouldn't interest you—deals, business matters."

"Oh!" She was silent, then, "What time do you have to go out?"

"Later."

"I could stay, keep the bed warm. I don't have to be up early, so if you liked I could stay all night. Yes?"

"Yeah—some other time, though."

Melanie's mouth tightened into a thin line. She was very beautiful and unused to turndowns. "You've got another girl," she accused. "That's it. You're going out to see someone else."

He sighed. They were all the same. They all wanted to own you. Why couldn't he find a woman who would keep her cool? He always chose very carefully. No hookers, junkies, or hustlers in any sense. He went out with black models, actresses, singers. Melanie, for instance, had recently been on the cover of *Cosmopolitan,* and the girl before her was a runner-up in the Miss Black America competition.

"Don't blow it," he hissed as she turned on the tears. "It ain't gonna work. Your lovely eyes gonna get all red and runny, and that I don't like."

"Shall I stay then?" she questioned tearfully.

Leroy shook his head. "I told you. Didn't I tell you? I got business to conduct."

Chapter 15

Rio attracted freaks the way a bitch in heat attracts dogs. They clustered around her in thrilled little groups, clad in outlandish clothes, high on anything that happened to be around, gossipy, bitchy.

Rio didn't mind. She could get it together with anyone as far as having a warm, generous relationship was concerned. She looked for the good in everyone, and if she didn't find it, she looked again.

Straight men were her only difficulty. Like Larry Bolding, for instance. She found they were all full of such ridiculous hang-ups, dishonesty, and bullshit. It turned her off. She became feline and hard in their company.

Rio had never been to London before, but she had friends eagerly awaiting her arrival. There was Peaches, the gloriously stunning blond model who had once been a man. And Perry Hernando, a gay Mexican singer who prowled London every so often looking for new talent. Rio had known them both in her Billy Express days.

They came to her rented apartment accompanied by a host of others. They brought champagne with them and smoked some incredible grass supplied by a middle-aged American lady in low-cut black. Then in cars and taxis they took Rio triumphantly to Tramp, the only place to go in London, according to Peaches and Hernando.

It was exactly where Rio wanted to be. Tramp, she'd found out, was the club where Angelo Bassalino put in a nightly appearance with his lady of the week.

After some deep-dish research she knew most of his movements and habits. At the moment he was currently screwing a bit-part actress, also a married woman with four children and a rich husband, and a female blackjack dealer from one of the casinos where he worked.

Angelo Bassalino liked women. Any shape, size, or color. He was not particular.

Rio had no set plan of action. She was confident that whatever she wished to do was possible. She knew people, and she knew she was able to get into their heads if she wanted to. It would be easy deciding what had to be done to destroy Angelo.

She wished she could have dealt with all three of Enzio Bassalino's sons—Frank, Nick, *and* Angelo. It was her plan. She should never have told anyone; she could have done it alone without any help. What did Lara and Beth know about beating someone mentally, reducing him to a wreck, finding the one chink and pressing, pressing until it gave way?

Bullshit! They knew how to get a guy in the sack and that was it. Not like Margaret; she could have done it. Margaret was capable of anything.

Rio remembered their first meeting. It was winter, and so cold she could recall how she'd first thought of setting her apartment building on fire. An insane thought, but at the time she was ready for any way to kill herself.

What a way to go! One big glorious blaze. But then she'd thought about all the other people living there, and what use would a good-bye note for Larry Bolding be if it went up in flames? She wanted him to suffer. Her plan was to ruin him and his whole stinking political career.

She had made her face up very carefully, an

extravaganza of exotic color. Then she'd put on a long red Halston dress. After all, she was a superstar—she certainly wasn't going to creep out.

She was high. A little acid to help her on the ultimate trip. By three o'clock in the morning she was ready to go. First some incredible sounds on the stereo—loud—then she'd used the razor that Larry kept at her place. He didn't like electric ones.

She slid the fresh blade out and cut a deep line along the inside of her right wrist, then her left. It didn't hurt; the sudden gush of blood was beautiful, it matched her dress.

She was laughing. It was the best she'd felt for months. No hang-ups, no worries, no anything.

She was still laughing when she passed out, the blood pumping out of her cut wrists onto the pure white carpet.

It was all hazy after that. Margaret's face, very close and concerned. A feeling of movement, of being carried. Voices—muffled and far away.

And after that the awakening—how many days later? Two? Three? Margaret Lawrence Brown sitting at a table writing, her long black hair propped back from a strong face by tinted glasses.

Rio couldn't move. She was in a strange bed

in a strange room, and her arms were bandaged up to the elbows.

"Hey," she managed, causing Margaret to look up at her, a direct-confrontation stare. She wore no makeup, and her face was not beautiful, not even pretty. But it was a face of such enormous warmth and attractiveness that Rio was immediately drawn to her. It was a strange feeling, because what the hell, she didn't even want to be in the world anymore.

Margaret smiled slightly and got up. Tall, small-bosomed in a loose T-shirt and Levi's. "I guess you're going to make it," she'd said in a gravelly voice. "It didn't look like it for a while, but I had a feeling you'd survive. I'm Margaret, I live next door, and I happened to get blasted out of bed by your musical choice. Since you're usually so quiet, I came over to investigate. You would have made a devastating picture for the newspapers—the red dress and the blood and the white rug. It was almost a shame to save you. Only think about it—you can't pull that kind of shit over a guy!" Margaret had shaken her head in disbelief. "Larry Bolding's an asshole. Baby, I don't even know him, but I'm here to tell you he's a prick. And we do not—I repeat, do *not*—kill ourselves over pricks."

Margaret never lost any time in making a point.

Rio stayed with Margaret in her apartment

for two weeks before moving back to her own place. She learned more in those two weeks than she had in a lifetime.

Margaret was that rare exception, a truly selfless person. She wanted nothing out of life except to do good for others. She gave her time, her energy, her money to any cause she found worthy. And she had a biting, furious anger at the way women were treated as second-class citizens. She wanted to change things, and she didn't just sit around talking about it like most people; she went out and did what she could.

In the dim recesses of Tramp Rio recognized Angelo Bassalino when he came in. She scrutinized him with a strong and steady gaze. He was with a skinny little blonde.

Rio had no plans to waste time. She walked directly over to his table and sat herself down.

"Hey, Angelo," she said tauntingly. "What's all this shit I hear about you being the best fuck in town?"

Chapter 16

Enzio Bassalino placed three phone calls. In order of importance he spoke to Frank in New York first.

"I'm thinking of coming in," he stated. "How's the climate?"

Frank realized his father was not referring to the weather. "The same," he replied, his voice guarded. He knew for a fact that the FBI had a tap on his phone.

"I'll come in anyway," Enzio growled. "The usual hotel, the usual setup—arrange it."

"It's not the right time." Frank tried to keep

the irritation out of his voice. Why did his goddamn father always have to interfere?

"I want to see the grandchildren." Enzio was stubborn. "At the same time we can clear up some other matters. You know what I mean?"

"Yeah. I know what you mean." Frank knew exactly what he meant. He meant the panic that was going on over the bombing of the Magic Lantern restaurant.

Frank had everything in hand. He was calling meetings and finding out hard facts. He didn't need any help.

At first he had thought Bosco Sam, or maybe the Crowns were responsible. But the information he'd collected pointed against them.

Tomassio Vitorelli, Frank's counselor, had been meeting with an informant at the Magic Lantern the night the bomb had exploded. Unfortunate for poor Tomassio.

"Okay, so arrange it. I'll be in tomorrow," Enzio said impatiently. "International, three o'clock. Tell Anna Maria to start cooking." He hung up, well aware that Frank was annoyed. Enzio knew his oldest son thought he could handle everything himself. But what was wrong with a little insurance? What was wrong with Enzio Bassalino showing his face in New York?

Enzio had found out the Crown gang were trying to move in on several Bassalino territories. They weren't succeeding, but they were causing certain problems. What with that and the protection business, he knew it was time he paid a visit. He was sure with him in town those problems would soon cease. Perhaps a personal meeting with Rizzo Crown would fix things. They went back many years together, so why not?

Finished with Frank, he telephoned Nick in Los Angeles. "What's happening?" he asked, always his opening question.

Nick gave him a short rundown.

"Fine, fine." Enzio coughed and spat into an ashtray on his desk, a habit that did not endear him to his staff. "I'm going to New York tomorrow—it might not be a bad idea for you to fly in for a couple of days. We'll have a family meeting."

"Why?" Nick didn't like leaving the Coast. He didn't like his suntan suffering for even one day.

"It might be advisable," Enzio said. "I'll let you know."

"Jesus," Nick muttered.

"What's the matter with you?" Enzio boomed. "Can't you leave the old broad for two days? What's she got, a direct line to your balls?"

"If it's necessary, I'll be there," Nick said, giving in without a fight. Maybe a trip to New York wasn't such a bad idea. It just might be the perfect opportunity to get something together with Lara that April couldn't find out about.

"Okay, okay, I'll let you know," Enzio said, hanging up.

Nick was a stupid boy. Any man was dumb if he let a woman tie his balls together. Enzio had always prided himself on being very clever about the female sex. A piece was a piece, and there was plenty around. "Use them before they use you" had always been his motto. Once they became clingy and demanding, that was the time to get rid of them.

Mary Ann August wriggled into his study. Clad in her customary bikini with puffs of teased blond hair, she stood silently picking off her nail polish until he said a curt "Yeah? What is it?"

"Alio's here," she singsonged. "Out by the pool. He wants a sandwich, and the cook's out. What shall I do?"

"So make him a sandwich," Enzio said irritably, delaying his call to Angelo.

"What kind?" she asked blankly.

"How the hell do I know? Ask him." Mary Ann was beginning to piss him off. Sometimes big boobs were not enough.

"There's cheese, I guess," she said vaguely. "Or cucumber. Do you think he'd like cucumber?"

"What am I? A chef?" Enzio stormed. "Get outta here, ya dumb broad. I gotta make a call."

Mary Ann left quickly. She knew when to make herself scarce.

It would have been nice, Enzio mused, if Rose had not gone insane and locked herself away. An old-style wife was irreplaceable. A woman who knew her position in life and kept it. It would have been far more convenient to stash his mistresses in separate apartments, visiting them only when necessary, putting up with their ridiculous chatter only when he had to.

But it was too lonely without anyone. He needed to share his bed. Sometimes he had nightmares, dreams from which he awoke shaking and cold around the heart. At those times he reached out for human contact; he desperately needed the security of another body nearby.

Enzio worried about his health. What if his heart should fail and no one was near? He had suffered one attack three years before. The doctors had assured him he was fine now, better than before.

Still . . . What did doctors know? He didn't trust any of them.

It wouldn't be a bad idea, he decided, to replace Mary Ann in New York. Her time was almost up.

Phoning London, he was aggravated because he could not get hold of Angelo. His son wasn't at the casino nor at his home. The boy was out screwing, Enzio thought with a snort. He smiled, the proud father. At Angelo's age he'd been just the same.

Ah . . . At Angelo's age he'd had the world by the balls. Prohibition, Chicago, a different kind of time, a world of crazy excitement and thrills. Once the Bassalino name had rated alongside Capone, Legs Diamond, O'Banion. Enzio sighed with pleasure when he remembered the early days with Alio by his side. It was all so different now, everything hidden under a cloak of legitimacy. Crime was getting dull.

Enzio chuckled and strolled out to the pool, still laughing. He wondered if Alio would remember the time they'd tried to bribe the chef of their favorite Italian restaurant. They'd wanted him to put arsenic in an archrival's soup. The chef had refused and fled the city, and to this day Enzio still missed the coward's incredible meatballs.

Chapter 17

They met on the plane like conspirators, Nick warily checking the first-class section for friends of his or April's. Only after he'd done this and found all was clear did he condescend to join Lara.

She was dressed all in white and looked ravishingly beautiful. He decided the risk was well worth taking, even though she'd steadfastly refused to meet him in Los Angeles, giving him an ultimatum—her or April.

There was no way he could possibly choose. He was going to *marry* April. Lara had turned up at the wrong time. Sure, he wanted to get her into bed, but he wasn't prepared to risk his future, and his future was most definitely April Crawford.

Enzio had suggested the New York trip at just the right moment. Nick mentioned to Lara he had to go and hinted she should come, too. Surprisingly, she'd said yes.

"April mustn't find out," he'd warned, and for a change she'd agreed with him.

"We'll do it your way," she'd said calmly.

Over the weeks they'd enjoyed an ongoing flirtation—bumping into each other at parties, restaurants, and clubs. The more he'd seen of her, the more he'd wanted her. Now he was going to get his wish.

He had the situation well covered. They'd arrived at the airport separately, boarded the plane separately, and they would disembark separately. Who could possibly find out they were traveling together?

Lara had her own apartment in New York. Nick planned to stay at the hotel with Enzio. He figured New York was a big place; you could get lost there. It wasn't a nosy little city like Los Angeles, where you couldn't even take a piss without everyone knowing.

All he wanted was a chance to be with Lara without the anxiety of April catching them together. One or two days should be long enough to get her out of his system. It was just sex—pure, unadulterated lust. Yeah, she was gorgeous, and well connected in her own way, but she wasn't April. April Crawford was a star. Something he had no intention of forgetting.

Frank was a demanding man. After the first night he came to Beth's room as soon as he arrived home. It was always late, and Anna Maria slept soundly.

He silenced Beth's objections, reassuring her that his wife was a heavy sleeper and would not wake up.

Beth accepted him in the dark, old-fashioned room above the kitchen. She accepted his kisses and embraces, the fumbling way he made love. In spite of the revulsion he produced in her, she felt sorry for him. Frank Bassalino stood for everything she loathed, and yet there was a certain loneliness in the man that caught her sympathy. Maybe it was the cruel joke nature had played on him; it made him vulnerable. It also explained why he needed a girl like her, a girl he thought was inexperienced, and who therefore could make no criticism or comparison.

She lived up to his expectations. She was soft, warm, and appreciative, feigning a childlike innocence that seemed to fascinate him.

He bought her little presents. One night a cheap charm bracelet, the next a pound of strawberries, which he proceeded to eat.

He was a selfish lover, satisfying himself and

forgetting about her. It never took him very long—a five-minute routine that didn't vary. He liked her to be in bed waiting. He insisted she wear her long white nightgown. First he would fondle her breasts for a few minutes, then suck at her nipples until he was ready to mount her. A few thrusts and it was over.

By the end of the week he was already talking of finding her an apartment.

By the end of the week she had already planned how she would arrange to have Anna Maria discover them together.

Lara called Cass as soon as she arrived at her apartment in New York. "I'm making progress," she said. "April should find out about us in the morning paper."

"Are you sure you're all right?" Cass asked anxiously.

"Perfect," Lara assured her confidently. "Once April discovers he flew here with me, he's out. The woman is too proud to accept seconds. The funny thing is I haven't slept with him." She paused. "How's Beth?"

"I don't know. I spoke to her and she seemed disturbed. I want her to quit. I told her so, but she won't listen. I'm worried."

"Yes, she's so young." Lara thought with concern of the sister she hardly knew. "I think we have to insist that she drop out of the whole thing. After all, she does have a child at the commune, and the important thing is to persuade her that little Chyna needs her more than our crazy scheme does."

"You're right," Cass agreed. "I'll try and make contact."

"And how about Rio? Any word from her?"

"A cable saying 'Success assured.' The agreement was to touch base every Wednesday. If I can't reach Beth by tomorrow, I'll go to the house and pretend I'm a relative."

"Good," Lara agreed. "Enzio Bassalino is in New York. That's the reason I'm here."

Cass sounded alarmed. "God, I hope Dukey doesn't find out. He's always muttering about there only being one way."

"Killing's too good for him," Lara said, surprised at her own coldness. "Our way is best."

She hung up, walked into the bathroom, brushed her luxuriant mane of hair, and touched up her makeup.

She looked tired, and she was worried about Beth. Her younger sister was such an innocent, so unworldly. Beth had been stuck away in a commune all her life, and now she was stuck in a house with a dangerous hood. Cass had to get her out, there was no question about it.

Next Lara thought about Nick. She was supposed to hate him, but it wasn't that easy. The funny thing was that instead of hating him she found she liked him—a pure, natural like that had nothing to do with money or position or title. God! It would certainly make everything a lot easier if she didn't. Still, she had a job to do. And with Beth out of the picture it was more important than ever.

Frank arrived at the hotel with Golli and Segal. They accompanied him everywhere; they were his protection, his insurance. The way things were going in New York, there was big trouble everywhere. Only the previous week one of his chief "executives" had been gunned down in the middle of Manhattan. He was taking no chances. Golli and Segal were worth the exorbitant money he paid them each week.

Enzio had used the hotel many times before, and his security arrangements were as usual. The entire third floor was inaccessible except to members of his immediate entourage. Even Frank had to use the complicated passwords, although all the men Enzio traveled with had known Frank since he was a baby.

Enzio did not believe in new faces. He kept a permanent army of twenty-five men who had been with him many years and were always on call. Frank had argued with him many times over this. "They're old guys, what can they do for you if there's trouble? They can barely carry a gun anymore, let alone use it."

Enzio laughed in his face. "These 'old guys,'

as you call them, are tougher and smarter than any of the punks you have around. I *know* I can't be got to—do you have the same security?"

Frank felt safe enough with Golli and Segal. They were young and fast—he'd seen them in action.

Father and son greeted each other warmly, kissing and hugging in the Italian way.

Enzio patted Frank on the shoulders, standing back to survey him. "So, you look okay," he announced. "How's the little girl? She about ready to pop again?" He was very fond of his daughter-in-law.

Frank nodded. "Anna Maria's fine. She's looking forward to seeing you." But his thoughts were not of his wife. His thoughts were of Beth.

"An' the bambinos? They excited to see their old grandpop?"

"Yeah, pa. Dinner tonight, Anna Maria's making your favorite—spaghetti, meatballs, the works."

"That's good." Enzio paused, his face becoming serious. "I'm most troubled by the reports I've been hearing."

Frank turned, staring out of the window. "Everything's under control," he said, his voice uptight.

"I wonder if Tomassio Vitorelli would agree with you," Enzio replied mildly, adding more harshly, "We're not gonna fuck around on this, Frank. I'm not here to get my rocks off." He frowned. "No use talkin' now. We'll discuss it tonight after dinner, when Nick is here."

"Sure." Frank managed a smile. "Sure, Poppa, everything's gonna be okay."

Chapter 18

Dukey K. Williams was pleased. The hit on the Magic Lantern restaurant was a success. It had disposed of Tomassio Vitorelli, a big man in the Bassalino organization. And the bombing had put the fear of God into other restaurants and clubs that didn't want the same treatment. Let the Bassalinos start to sweat. It was a good beginning.

Leroy Jesus Bauls was also pleased. The hit had been his idea.

Dukey K. Williams had come to him.

Dukey K. Williams was prepared to let him do it his way.

Dukey K. Williams was going to lay a lot of bucks on Leroy. Mucho, mucho big bucks.

Yeah, things were sweet for a guy who had started out with everything against him.

Leroy's Swedish mother was a hooker, and his black father a pimp. As soon as he was able he'd left home. His parents were dead as far as he was concerned, and it wouldn't bother him one bit if they actually were.

Good-looking at an early age, he never had any trouble finding a bed to sleep in. If he'd wanted to, he could have followed his father's profession; there were plenty of offers. But Leroy had no desire to be beholden to any woman.

Instead he joined a street gang and cruised with them for a while. It was small stuff, rolling drunks and old ladies, knocking off neighborhood stores. By the time the profits were split up they were practically nonexistent. Leroy knew he had to move on to better things.

He decided that narcotics was the business for him. Once or twice he'd smoked pot, tried acid twice. Neither did anything for him. That was good. The thing to be when dealing with drugs was cool, and definitely a nonparticipant.

He'd seen what drugs did to people, the way dope affected their looks, and he wanted none of that. But pushing was another bag of shit; pushing could lead to a lot of money.

Leroy was young, good-looking, and a convincing talker. He picked out the area he wanted to operate and, with a small stake from a friend, went into business.

Soon he found he was stepping on toes. The space he'd picked was already fully covered. They warned him off. They thought he was some punk kid, easy to handle. He bought a gun with his first week's profits and waited.

There were three sets of toes he was stepping on. Within a month all three of them were dead, shot. Leroy wrapped his gun in plastic, weighted it with rocks, and safely laid it to rest at the bottom of the river.

With his fifth week's profits he bought himself another one. He was sixteen years old.

For a year he concentrated solely on dealing, working on his own with good sources of supply. He stashed his money away and kept his gun handy. Nobody bothered him. His reputation preceded him. He kept to his own area and didn't get in anyone's way.

He lived alone in a rooming house. Never went out except on business and rarely spent any money. By the end of a year he'd saved a substantial amount. Enough to buy a car and a whole new wardrobe of clothes, and to rent a decent apartment.

His first purchase was a black Mercedes. Next he had several black suits custom-made for him. And then he furnished his apartment with a lot of expensive black leather couches and chairs.

He looked older than seventeen.

Leroy found that to maintain his new life-style he needed even more money. So he employed two friends of his to work his space and moved on to new territory.

Within days he received word that Bosco Sam wanted to see him. Bosco Sam's toes were too many to step on and Leroy knew it, so he paid him a visit.

They came to an arrangement. Leroy was to keep to the area he already had, and instead of moving in on Bosco Sam's action, Bosco Sam would throw a couple of things his way that would bring him a lot more money than hustling drugs.

Leroy liked the idea. More bucks for less work, and he still kept a couple of guys working for him.

In the first year Bosco Sam gave him three contracts to take care of. Three hits. Leroy executed them all without a hitch.

Leroy was moving up. He was getting himself a reputation, and it was doing him nothing but good.

Now, four years later, Leroy Jesus Bauls was

top man in his profession. He had long ago moved out of the drug scene.

He had used his spare time to study explosives, electronics, computer bombs. There was nothing he didn't know how to do, from blowing up a plane to planting a bomb in a bank that he could detonate three weeks later.

Leroy Jesus Bauls was a free-lance hit man. The best.

He had a reputation for taking risks, and every risk he had ever taken had paid off. Leroy was riding high.

Now he waited. Dukey K. Williams would let him know when to move again, and when he did, Leroy would be ready.

Chapter 19

Angelo's apartment in Mayfair was small. A living room, kitchen, and bathroom. He'd splashed out on the bedroom. The walls were draped with leopard and tiger skins, the floor was carpeted in three-inch-thick fur, the ceiling was a kaleidoscope of different-colored mirrors. Naturally, the bed dominated. It did everything electrically, from turning around in a slow circle to producing television, stereo, or coffee at the touch of a button.

Angelo was proud of his domain. "Hot, huh?" he boasted to Rio.

She dismissed her surroundings with a

glance. "Get yourself a water bed, baby" was her only comment.

They were both stoned. After Rio's initial introductory remark to Angelo he'd lost no time in getting rid of his blond companion and joining up with Rio's group. She was immediately cool, palming him off on Peaches while making rude comments about cocky Italian studs.

As usual, Rio was the center of attention, outrageous in whore's shoes with five-inch heels that raised her six-foot height to ridiculous proportions. She towered over everybody, her sinewy body undulating on the packed dance floor in a revealing dress tied and swathed around her body. Silver bangles jangled halfway up both her arms, and fertility symbols jostled and moved around her neck. Her makeup was extreme, while her long black Indian hair was coiled up and hidden under a purple Afro wig.

She danced with everyone, generating sexuality and excitement at high-level voltage.

Angelo was content to hang around and watch. He had no doubts that later she'd go home with him.

He sat back and enjoyed the show, remembering a few years earlier. New York. At the time he'd been working for his brother Frank, and one day he'd been sent over to Billy Express's house to deliver a package. "Personally," Frank had said. "Make sure you give it to him *personally.*"

Billy Express was not home, and Angelo had been told to wait. He hadn't enjoyed being treated like a messenger boy. It pissed him off. But then he heard the noises, unmistakable noises, and he went to investigate, soft-footed in the white sneakers he always chose to wear.

The noises came from the room next to the study where he'd been told to wait. Opening the door a crack, he peered in.

Rio Java and a Chinese man were performing on the floor. She was naked, spread-eagled, and above her the Chinese posed very still while she groaned loudly. Occasionally the Chinese man moved, grinding himself deeply into her, withdrawing, and then remaining motionless until the next short stab. It was driving Rio mad, until suddenly she'd clutched at him, locking her extra-long legs around his neck and screaming with complete abandon.

Angelo had closed the door quickly, feeling more than horny. As soon as he'd delivered the package to Billy Express he'd hurried over to Carita's house and dropped another load.

"You bin here four times this week," Carita had complained. "I told Frank you could have two freebies a week. Whadda ya think I am, for chrissake? I'm running a business, not a friggin' charity!"

The memory had always remained with

Angelo. And now Rio Java was in London, in his apartment, and he was just as horny as the day he'd delivered the package to Billy Express.

Rio stretched, touched a strap or two, and with a couple of deft moves her dress fell off. She wore nothing else except the hooker shoes and the purple wig. She was very thin, almost bony, almost flat-chested, with incredible black extended nipples. In underground movie circles her nipples were famous, having been photographed by Billy Express from every angle. In fact, her nipples were almost as famous as Andy Warhol's Campbell's soup can.

Angelo hurriedly stripped off his clothes, eager to keep up. Then he lowered the lights to a red glow and flicked on a James Brown tape.

Rio's eyes swept over him, lingering on his most important asset. "Is that it?" she asked with an amused laugh.

Angelo grinned unsurely, not quite certain what she meant. She couldn't possibly mean he was underendowed. He had a good, solid hard-on. Usually he received nothing but admiring oohs and aahs, not short, derisive laughs.

"Well now, *little* boy," she said mockingly. "Where would you like to begin?"

Angelo approached her, silently wishing she would take her shoes off. Without the goddamn shoes they would be more or less the same height. As it was, the shoes gave her an advantage he didn't like. They made him feel small.

Rio moved her body in time to the music, parting her legs, swaying back and forth to the funky sounds of James Brown's "Sex Machine."

"Hey," he said, "take your shoes off."

"But honey-pie, I *looove* my shoes," she sighed in an exaggerated Southern accent. "They make me feel *reeal* big and mean. All the better to eat up naughty *little* boys like Angelo Bassalino."

He gripped her by the waist.

"Show me your stuff, super stud," she drawled.

They moved together.

"Get up—get on up—get up—get on up—get up—get on up—stay on the scene—get on up—like a sex machine." Rio sang along with James Brown while Angelo's grip tightened and he managed to move her over to the bed. She was still singing as he pushed her back. "Get on up," she chanted, "get up—get it together—right on, baby."

He mounted her, and before he knew what was happening she stretched her long legs straight out, trapping him inside her, and with one movement she twisted her pelvis up, and the pressure was so great, so incredibly tight, that he came at once.

She started to laugh, loud, mocking laughter. The whole thing had only taken a few seconds.

"Hey, baby, baby," she crooned. "What are you—a rabbit?"

She dissolved with more laughter while Angelo withdrew and tried to puzzle out what had happened. All he'd done was move inside her and that was it, a viselike grip on his manhood that pumped it all out of him in one fell swoop. Jesus! What was going on here?

Rio rolled across the bed. "How long's the intermission?" she complained, throwing off her purple wig and shaking her long, shiny black hair free.

To his credit, Angelo was hard again. He prided himself on his control, knowing he could go for hours if it was required. Mind over matter, that was the secret. And his mind had probably been dwelling on the first time he'd seen her.

He moved over her breasts with his tongue.

"Let's fuck, baby," she said briskly. "I'm here for action. We can worry about tongue jobs later."

She rolled on her stomach and he entered her from behind. When he was good and in she drew her legs together and raised herself a few inches. Again there was that incredible sensation, a tightness so relentless he couldn't stop himself from coming. And it was a great come, a beautiful happening that no amount of mind over matter could stop.

"Jesus!" she exclaimed angrily. "How long is it since you've been laid?"

Angelo was exhausted. He lay back on the bed in a daze, closing his eyes. Five minutes of sleep and he'd feel strong again.

James Brown sang "It's a Man's Man's Man's World."

Angelo slept.

Grinning to herself, Rio got up and slipped into her dress. It was a satisfying start.

Jamming on her wig, she danced around the room in her hooker shoes, humming softly to herself. Then in brown lipstick she wrote on the bathroom mirror: *HONEY*, YOU'VE *GOT* TO BE KIDDING!!

She let herself out without disturbing him.

Chapter 20

Mary Ann August was delighted Enzio had decided to bring her to New York with him. She would never admit it—well, only to herself—but she found Miami tediously boring. It wasn't so much Miami, but the fact that she wasn't allowed out on her own, and that the people who came to the house were all old. And then of course there was the woman peering out of the window all the time. It was very unnerving to have a pair of crazed black eyes following you everywhere.

"Who is it?" Mary Ann had asked in alarm when she'd first arrived.

"Forget it," Enzio had warned her. "Just ignore it, an' *never* let me catch your ass near that room. You understand me?"

Mary Ann knew enough not to question him any further, but that didn't stop her speaking to the maid who took meals into the room twice a day.

The maid was Italian and frightened to talk, but gradually Mary Ann pieced together the story. The woman was Enzio's wife. She was a mental case and never left her room.

Mary Ann was scared, but as the weeks drifted into months she forgot about the crazy, ever-watchful eyes and pretended they weren't there. It was kind, she reflected, that Enzio let the old bag stay and had not shoved her into an institution.

Mary Ann planned to do lots of things in New York. She wanted to buy new clothes, see all the Broadway shows, and eat at the best restaurants.

Enzio had other ideas. Upon their arrival he shut her in the hotel suite and told her to stay there until he said otherwise.

They had arrived in the morning; now it was seven in the evening, and Mary Ann was bored, hungry, and fed up.

She sat pouting on the bed, legs crossed, china-blue eyes glued to a game show on the television.

At first she didn't hear the knock on the door,

and she was quite startled when Alio Marcusi walked in.

"Oh, it's you," she said, her voice sulky. "Where's Enzio?"

Alio smiled. He had showered and put on his new blue suit. His few remaining hairs were plastered down with a shiny pomade.

Enzio had given him the word. Mary Ann August was out. There was a position for her in Los Angeles.

Enzio always allowed Alio a turn when he was finished with a girl. It had been that way for thirty years. Sometimes they objected. Those were the ones Alio liked best. At his age it was difficult getting it up under normal circumstances.

"He won't be coming," Alio said mildly. "I have a message for you, my dear."

Chapter 21

There were candles on the table at Frank Bassalino's house. His children, washed, scrubbed and clad in their best clothes, sat straight-backed at the table. Frank had given up his place at the head to his father and settled himself on Enzio's right. Anna Maria nervously faced her husband.

Nick was there, laughing and joking with the two younger children. He'd wanted to spend the evening with Lara, but Enzio had insisted he attend the dinner, and his father was not a man you argued with.

He'd arranged to meet Lara later. She hadn't

minded, merely smiled and said, "I understand, Nick. Family is family."

April would have ranted and raved for a week.

"Hey," Enzio roared. "Anna Maria makes the best spaghetti in town. You're a lucky man, Frank, you know that, huh?" He paused, belching loudly. "Of course, *I* could give her a few hints about the sauce. A little more garlic, stronger wine . . ."

Anna Maria giggled timidly.

Frank glanced at Beth. She had entered the room to assist the youngest child with his food. Her long hair was tied off her face, and she looked pale. He wondered how quickly Anna Maria would fall asleep tonight, and how long before he could be with Beth.

A nerve throbbed in his cheek. There would be business to discuss after dinner; it could turn out to be a lengthy evening.

After dessert and coffee Enzio sent Anna Maria and the children from the room. "Men's talk," he explained with a wink, sipping from a small glass of Sambuca.

When he began to speak his eyes fixed firmly on Frank. "It doesn't take long," he said sourly, his good humor evaporating, "for the word to get around when you got no balls."

"What?" Frank jumped, feeling anger and frustration flood through his body.

"In our business, somebody throws a hit on

you, you shove it right back at 'em. You don't fuck around. No way."

"I've been lookin' to find out who's responsible," Frank replied, his voice a surly mutter.

"Fuck that!" Suddenly Enzio was screaming. "Who gives a shit 'bout who's to blame? What you do is pile some action on *all* the fuckers—you'll hit the dirt with one of 'em. Huh? Listen to an old man, Frankie boy—Don't let nobody shit on you. 'Cos if you do, we'll all end up under the pile."

Lara prowled around her apartment like a stranger. She hated the draped paisley fabric ceiling, the matching walls, the small round table with a collection of interesting miniature boxes.

She loathed the exotic plants climbing up the antique-mirrored hall. She couldn't stand the zebra throw rugs, the brown leather couches.

Her apartment had been designed by a decorator; there were no personal touches. About the only place she felt at home was the bathroom. Here, among the rows of makeup, atomizers, and brushes, she could relax.

The apartment had been put together with a view to looking sensational in the fashion and beautiful-home magazines. And indeed it did.

Lara had spent more time being photographed in it than living there.

She decided that when the whole business with Nick was over she would sell it. It was pointless to surround oneself with somebody else's idea of good taste.

When *would* the whole business with Nick be over? Wasn't it just beginning?

Sometimes she felt so confused. Was the revenge going to work? If April Crawford left Nick, was it going to affect him *that* much? And after she'd consoled him for a few weeks, when *she* dumped him, what then? Even if he was destroyed, how was that really going to punish Enzio Bassalino?

She gave a deep sigh. At the time Rio's revenge had sounded perfect. But now . . . well, she wasn't so sure anymore. Maybe Dukey was the one with the right ideas.

Slowly she dressed to meet Nick at Le Club. A black jersey snake of a dress with no back. A jeweled choker from Afghanistan. Bracelets of thin beaten silver halfway up her arm.

Tonight was the night. Take Mr. Nick Bassalino home to bed and keep him there until he read the morning gossip columns. The longer it took for him to call April the better.

Another sigh. Margaret wouldn't have approved of what they were trying to do. Margaret would have been ashamed of their resorting to sex to get what they wanted.

The phone rang. She picked it up.

"Lara? Lara, is that you?" The anxious voice of Prince Alfredo Masserini.

"Oh, Alfredo. How did you know I was here?"

"I call you every day," he said indignantly. "Every day I try. Every day no answer. How do you think I feel?"

"I'm sorry. I had to fly out to the Coast. I just got back." She wasn't sorry at all. The break was delightful.

"But Lara, Lara," he accused, "you could have phoned me."

"I said I'm sorry," she snapped.

"Now I have you, so we forget it." The prince sensibly realized arguing was not going to get him anywhere. "You want I come there?"

"No."

"So you fly to me then. Tomorrow. I meet you at Rome airport, then together we go to Gstaad for the backgammon. Yes, my darling?"

"No, Alfredo. I have business to finish."

"Ah, Lara, my beautiful. You make me very wild."

"Give me a few more days. I'll join you in Gstaad."

"How many days?"

"Don't pin me down. Phone me tomorrow."

She hung up quickly, ignoring the phone

when it immediately began to ring again. Alfredo had been a spoiled Italian prince all his life; it would do him good to strike out for once.

Besides, she didn't want to be late for Nick.

Chapter 22

Angelo called Rio ten times before he finally reached her.

"Hey," he said, "about the other night."

"No apologies," Rio said with a deep, throaty laugh. "I understand, I'm a *veree* understanding lady."

"Maybe we can get together tonight?"

"Honey, understanding I may be, but you and I just don't swing at the same pace."

"Hey—the other night was a mistake," he explained. "That's not usually the way I am. I don't want to boast, but—"

She cut him short. "You're a sweet, horny

little guy, and great for teenyboppers and cute little bunnies who want some fast—and I *do* mean fast—action. But sweetheart, you and I are in different leagues."

Angelo felt his whole reputation was at stake. "I can explain about the other night. It was—"

She interrupted him again. "Yeah, baby, it certainly was." And then she cut him off.

He threw the phone down in disgust. How dare that great big freak put him down like this? He wanted to see her, to prove his manhood. It was a slight to have her think of him as a sexual failure. Shit! He was a *great* fuck. Countless women could confirm that. He could go for hours. He had incredible control.

Picking up the phone, he dialed his married lady friend. "Come on over right now," he commanded.

"I can't, one of the children is sick," the woman apologized.

He slammed the phone down. Was he losing his touch?

Next he reached his female croupier friend. She arrived within the hour, and he rushed her into bed, giving her controlled action and countless orgasms for two hours. She screamed and moaned her appreciation. He found he couldn't come himself. He was still hard when he threw her out.

He phoned Rio again.

"Wow, you're a very anxious *little* boy," she

said mockingly. "I don't like anxious guys. You know something, honey? It *really* turns me off."

"Can I come over?" he asked, hating himself for begging, but consumed with the need to prove himself to her.

She consulted her watch; it was six o'clock. "Okay. Be here in five minutes."

As soon as she put the phone down she went out.

Angelo hurried over and then waited outside her rented apartment for an hour, constantly pressing the buzzer. Naturally, there was no reply, which really pissed him off. Just who did the bitch think she was?

Finally he settled himself in at a nearby bar and had a few drinks. Every fifteen minutes he phoned her, getting no answer.

He consumed several Scotches. Normally he didn't drink much; grass was his scene. But tonight he needed something.

By the time he arrived at the casino he was unsteady on his feet and belligerent. Eddie Ferrantino took one look and sent him home.

He called up another girlfriend and met her at Tramp. Rio was there, surrounded by her so-called friends.

"You're a fuckin' bitch," he hissed at her.

"And you're a lousy lay," she hissed back.

"Listen, lady—come home with me now and

you'll eat your words," he insisted, forgetting about his girlfriend.

"It's not *words* I'm interested in eating," she said with a mocking grin.

"It's not words you'll get," he mumbled, wishing he was sober.

"Let's go," she said briskly.

They took a taxi. Rio flung off her clothes as soon as they entered his apartment.

Angelo realized he'd made a mistake. The booze had made his body limp and his mind groggy.

"Well?" She faced him, hands on hips, legs spread. "Get your clothes off, lover. Let's *see* what you can do."

She stripped him herself. He couldn't have summoned a hard-on if his life depended on it. Humiliation overcame him.

Laughingly she jeered, "Call Momma when you grow up to be a *big* boy. Okay, babe?"

And with that she dressed and left.

Chapter 23

It was late by the time Nick was through at his brother Frank's house. There were problems on top of problems. And a lot of talk. Nick didn't feel he was that much involved. Things were running smoothly for him in California; the inside killings and takeovers in New York didn't really concern him.

"Putan!" Enzio spat at him when he said as much. "What happens here today happens there tomorrow. You think you're protected by some fuckin' guardian angel? Balls!"

Both Enzio and Frank were mad at him because he had flown in with no bodyguard.

"You don't *move* in New York unless you're covered," Enzio had bellowed, and Frank immediately agreed. They'd dismissed the car and chauffeur he'd rented at the airport and replaced it with a black Cadillac sedan and two of Frank's men.

Nick couldn't help wondering how Lara was going to feel about a couple of heavies stationed outside her front door when they were together.

He arrived at Le Club late. Lara was with a group he fortunately didn't know. To his annoyance, she introduced him. He wished she hadn't.

Glancing around, he couldn't spot any familiar faces. What a relief! Anyway, it wasn't like he was *alone* with Lara. How could anyone think they were together? He'd even arrived after her.

Relaxing slightly, he decided she looked more beautiful than ever. Immediately he wanted to touch and hold her. Why waste time? He was sick of being with her only at parties and discotheques.

"Why don't we get out of here, beautiful lady?" he suggested in a low voice, touching her leg under the table.

"You just got here," she chided gently. "It's rude."

"Listen." His grip tightened on her leg. "I don't give a damn. How about you?"

"Don't you?" She sounded amused. "My,

how the climate changes your attitude. Shall we dance?"

He didn't feel like dancing. He just wanted to be alone with her.

Reluctantly, he allowed himself to be pulled onto the dance floor, where she pressed against him. Once again he felt the excitement and the promise of what was to come.

The hell with April. He was free to do what he pleased. He wasn't married yet.

There was an Italian restaurant called Pinocchios in New York that reserved a king's welcome for Enzio Bassalino whenever he was in town. It was a family concern. Mother, father, two daughters, and a son. They anticipated Enzio's needs, and on any evening he dropped by, nearby tables were given only to people he personally approved.

At one such table sat Kosta Gennas. A small, sweating man with blackened teeth and gnarled skin. It seemed incongruous that he should be sitting with the three most attractive girls in the room.

Kosta chewed on the end of a stubby cigar and sucked at his Scotch through a special silver straw.

No one at the table spoke. The girls, three different kinds of beauties, stared vacantly ahead. They all had old-fashioned teased hairstyles, although they each had hair of a different shade. They were all big of bosom, long of leg.

Kosta Gennas jumped up abruptly when Enzio Bassalino entered the restaurant.

Enzio nodded briefly at him as he passed his table. But it wasn't until an hour later that he summoned Kosta to join him. "I like the look of the blonde," Enzio said. "What's her story?"

"She's nineteen years old," Kosta replied quickly. "A lovely girl, hard worker, only been with us two months. She was married to some bum, and when he split on her she decided there were smarter ways to make a living. We was saving her to send to Brazil—she'd be a sensation there. Of course, when I heard you was lookin', we hung on to her."

"Is she clean?" Enzio asked, getting straight to the point.

"Is she clean?" Kosta echoed in amazement, his furtive eyes darting around in surprise at Enzio's six or seven male companions. "He asks me if she's clean. Would I ever—"

"Enough," Enzio interrupted sharply. He didn't like Kosta Gennas, never had. But Kosta had the best girls, and he always knew exactly which ones would please Enzio the most. "Send her over," he growled. "I'll see for myself."

The girl wobbled across the restaurant on

ridiculous stiletto heels. She stood by the side of the table, grinning foolishly, until Enzio indicated she should sit beside him.

When she was seated he looked her over closely. She had a pretty, pointed face, dominated by jammy, wide red lips. Blue-shadowed gray eyes, a smattering of freckles she'd endeavored to conceal, and—from what he could see—a perfect body.

"What's your name, dear?" he asked kindly, patting her on the knee in a not-so-fatherly way.

"Miriam," she whispered, in a breathy Marilyn Monroe voice.

"Well, Miriam," he said, his eyes greedily devouring her ample cleavage, "how would you feel about comin' to stay at my house in Miami?"

Anna Maria set her alarm clock for six A.M. every day. Then, heavy with child, she would stumble in the dark to the kitchen, where she liked to sit and drink warm, sweet tea, and watch the morning grow light.

Anna Maria had never trusted anyone else to make her children's breakfast. She enjoyed doing it herself. Mixing the hot, lumpy porridge. Heating the bread. Setting out the homemade plum jam. By seven, when they all appeared, she always had everything ready.

Anna Maria was a strong girl, but after four

pregnancies her legs were feeling weak, her belly stretched almost beyond control. She was hoping the birth would be soon. Frank went off her when she was pregnant. He never touched her and avoided looking at her. Not that he said anything, but she knew, and it saddened her. After all, Frank was the one who wanted many children.

Anna Maria struggled into her robe. She was exhausted; she hoped today would be the day. It was a strain entertaining Frank's father. There had been so much extra cooking to do, preparing all his favorite dishes. And the children always became more excitable than usual, while Frank himself was surly and gruff.

It seemed as if she'd just gotten into bed, and now it was another day. Wearily she plodded into the kitchen, switched on the light, and stared with a sense of unreality at her husband.

Frank was crouched over Beth, who he had spread-eagled across the kitchen table. His face was creased with concentration, and his breath was short. He was dressed, but Beth was naked, a crumpled white nightgown lying on the floor by her feet.

Anna Maria's hand fled to the crucifix she wore around her neck, and, her eyes wide with shock, she began to mumble in Italian.

"Jesus Christ!" Frank bellowed. He was nearing the moment of climax and was in no mood to be interrupted.

Beth wriggled out from under him. It was too late for him to stop. With a roar of fury he came all over the kitchen floor. The final insult.

"You fuckin' bitch," he screamed at Anna Maria. "What the hell you doin' spyin' on me?" His face was red with rage.

Anna Maria turned to run, but it was too late. Frank was after her, his arm raised in uncontrollable anger. He struck her across the face twice. The second time she fell to the floor.

"Bitch!" he yelled, standing over her with his arm raised, ready to give her more punishment.

Beth could not believe what was happening. She hadn't meant it to be like this. When she'd altered the time on Anna Maria's alarm clock she'd fully intended that Anna Maria would discover them together. But she hadn't realized Frank would turn into a screaming madman.

For a moment she was paralyzed. And then the full realization of what he was doing to his wife hit her. With all her strength she threw herself at him, trying to hold back the angry blows now raining down on Anna Maria.

He shoved her away.

"Stop it, Frank. Stop it!" she screamed. "You're killing her!"

Suddenly he seemed to realize what he was doing. Abruptly he stopped and began to groan. "Oh, my God. Oh, Jesus! What have I done?"

Anna Maria lay very still. For a moment Beth

feared she might be dead. But she listened and heard faint breathing, and without a word to Frank she rushed to the phone and called an ambulance.

Frank was crying and trying to cradle Anna Maria in his arms when the ambulance arrived.

"She fell down the stairs," he told the ambulance attendants. "I couldn't save her. She fell."

The two men exchanged glances. They'd heard that one before.

Then Anna Maria started to groan. Horrible, loud, animal groans.

"Please! Get her to the hospital quickly," Beth said urgently. "I think she's starting to have the baby."

Chapter 24

Leroy Jesus Bauls watched the ambulance pull up at Frank Bassalino's house in the early hours of the morning with hardly a flicker of interest showing in his flat eyes. He was chewing gum, slowly, methodically. Now he took the gum from his mouth, squeezed it into a tight, hard ball, and rolled it between his fingers.

How easy it would be to lay a hit on Frank Bassalino. One carefully aimed shot between the eyes—it would be a cinch. By the time the two goons who were apparently his protection reacted, Leroy Jesus Bauls would be long gone.

Frank Bassalino was a far easier target than the old man. Enzio Bassalino knew what protection was all about, and wherever he went he made sure he was always surrounded and shielded. Of course, he protected himself in the old-fashioned way. Somebody should tell him, Leroy thought, with a wide yawn.

It was a shame there was nothing to be done right now. But he'd studied his homework, and if the occasion arose, if Dukey K. Williams gave the word for the final hit . . . Well, he was ready.

Leroy dropped his chewing gum to the ground. He had work to do. The Bassalinos were proving to be a stubborn family, but they would learn . . . eventually.

Later that morning Leroy walked slowly toward the van he had stolen. He wore cheap clothes with SAMSONS LINENS written across the T-shirt he had on. Once in the van he jammed on a black leather cap and yellow-tinted shades.

With a tight smile he imagined he could hear the witnesses now. "Yeah—a black boy—about twenty-something—tall, skinny—how the hell do I know what he looked like—he was *black*."

"Sure, sure. We all look alike, baby," he muttered to himself. *"Beee-oootiful!"*

He drove the van carefully. It wouldn't do to have any kind of accident.

Barberellis was a large Italian restaurant and bar situated on a main street. Pulling the van up outside, Leroy got out. Collecting a large laundry basket from the back of the van, he carried it inside.

A girl was sitting behind a cash register adding up bills, while a wizened old man beat at the floor listlessly with a broom.

"Morning," Leroy sang out. "Samsons Linens, fresh delivery. Anything to go?"

The girl looked up vaguely. She had only worked there a week. "I don't know," she said. "Nobody's in yet. You'd better leave it on a table."

"Sure." Whistling, he chose a table by the window. The old man kept on sweeping. "I'll drop by tomorrow," Leroy said cheerfully.

"Okay," the girl replied, disinterested.

Still whistling, he departed.

Leroy was three blocks away when he heard the explosion. It gave him a strange, almost sensual jolt of pleasure.

Carefully he extracted a new piece of gum from the pack, and even more carefully he drove the van to his next stop.

Manny's was a nightclub, and the front was all closed up. Leroy took another laundry basket from the van and made his way around the back. There was an open door, but no one around.

Leroy began to whistle as he carried the basket past several dirty-looking dressing rooms, across the dance floor, and placed it on a table.

He was starting to perspire slightly, the basket was heavy, and there wasn't that much time. He was cutting it close.

Quickly he turned to leave, and as he did so the door to the ladies' room swung open. A sharp voice said, "Hey, boy, what you think you doin' here?"

Leroy stopped and smiled. "Samsons Linens," he said politely.

A fat old black woman waddled into sight. Obviously she was the cleaner. With her was a small, bright-eyed black child.

"We don' deal with no Samsons Linens," the old woman said with an impatient snort. "So you all kin git that basket outta here fast as you got it in. Unnerstand me, boy?"

He glanced at his watch. *Shit!* a voice screamed in his head. *Shit! Shit! Shit! Be smart and get your ass out.*

But something made him hesitate. He couldn't leave them. They were his people.

Jesus! What was the matter with him? Was he getting soft?

"Well, ma'am," he said calmly, "if you'll be kind enough to step outside with me, maybe you can tell that to the driver, 'cos he ain't gonna listen to me."

The old woman viewed him suspiciously, then she said to the child, "You stay here, Vera May. Don't you touch nothin', you hear?"

Christ! Now he was really sweating. Time was running out, and what could he do? Tell the truth? No, the old crone wouldn't believe him. Anyway, there wasn't time.

On impulse he scooped the kid up and started to run back the way he had come in. The child began to yell.

Leroy glanced behind him. Waving her arms in a panic, the old woman careened after them.

In his head he began the countdown—*sixty, fifty-nine, fifty-eight.* There was no time to take the van now. It would have to go up with the rest of the building. *Forty-five, forty-four, forty-three.* Outside at last.

"Shut up," he muttered to the screaming kid. The old woman would be out soon. Get at least a block away.

He ran down the street clutching the child, and behind him he heard the old woman screeching, "Stop that man, stop him—he's got my Vera May, my baby!"

Passersby turned to look at him, but nobody tried to detain him. This was New York; people were not stupid.

At the corner he paused. Any second now.

He placed the child on the pavement. "You stay right here," he commanded.

In the distance he saw the old woman getting closer.

Without hesitating he sprinted off in the direction of the subway entrance, annoyed at his own foolishness.

Within seconds he heard the explosion. Glancing back, he noticed the woman and kid were together, frozen in shock, while people around them ran back toward the noise.

Ducking down the stairs to the subway, he went straight to the men's room, where he got rid of the Samsons Linens T-shirt, the hat, and the shades.

It had been a good morning's work. It would certainly scare the shit out of the Bassalino family. And Dukey K. Williams would be more than pleased.

Leroy was satisfied. Nobody could beat him when it came to doing things right.

Chapter 25

Angelo didn't know what it was. It was a feeling that twisted his gut and stayed in his head. Rio Java. Rio Java. All he could think about was Rio Java.

Was this love? he thought to himself bitterly.

This couldn't be love, this nagging, persistent obsession.

Rio Java was not a beautiful woman; she wasn't even a particularly young woman. She was just a freak. A tall, randy, red Indian fuckin' freak.

He made up his mind to forget her.

Enzio phoned from New York to inform him

there was trouble all over, there had been certain threats. It was best that Angelo not go around unprotected.

"Aw, c'mon," Angelo bitched. "Nobody's gonna come after me." His father talked like an old gangster movie.

"Read the newspapers, you dumb little cocksucker, there's hits happenin' everywhere. You're my son, so that makes you a target. I'm havin' the Stevestos assign a man to you."

Angelo groaned. "Listen—"

"No, *you* listen," Enzio said coldly. "I'm gettin' reports of you being drunk, bumming around. Straighten your ass or I'll haul you back here. You want that?"

Angelo swallowed an angry reply. He liked it in London. The more distance between himself and his family the better. "Okay, okay. I'll get myself together," he promised.

"You'd better," Enzio warned.

A man called Shifty Fly was commissioned to protect him. It infuriated Angelo that he had to be followed and accompanied everywhere.

Shifty Fly looked like his name. He was small, with watery, darting eyes and a thin, downturned mouth. Under the crabby gray suit he wore rested a shoulder holster and a concealed gun.

"This is a joke," Angelo complained to Eddie Ferrantino.

Eddie's cold eyes flicked over Angelo, marveling yet again that this bearded asshole was Enzio Bassalino's son. "Just do as your father says, be a good little boy, huh?"

Fuck the "little boy" jazz. Angelo was sick of it. First Rio and now Eddie. Who the frig did they think they were?

He took out his various girlfriends and gave it to them regularly. There were no complaints.

He forced himself not to contact Rio. She was a bad scene, and even he knew enough not to ask for more.

He couldn't hold out. He called her.

"Hey, Rio, this is Angelo."

"Angelo who?"

Bitch! "Angelo Bassalino."

Her voice was cool. "Let me see now, I don't think I remember an Angelo Bassalino. . . ."

He laughed, full of false bravado. "Stop kidding around. I thought you might like dinner."

"I *always* like dinner. In fact, I have it every night." A long pause. "Do *you* have it every night?"

"Yeah."

"Then why don't you run off and have it now?"

She hung up on him. The bitch hung up!

He sent her flowers, something he had *never* done. She sent them back when they were dead with a short note: "Hey—isn't it funny—does everything you handle go limp?"

He found that although he was able to service all his girlfriends, it was virtually impossible for him to reach a climax. He remained hard as a rock, ready to go forever, never reaching the final destination. It was causing him great physical discomfort. When the hard-on vanished he was left with a pain in his gut that lasted all night.

Apart from that aggravation, there was Shifty Fly always close at hand. Foul-mouthed and slimy, he trailed Angelo everywhere.

Rio was pleased with the way things were going. She'd always possessed the power of grabbing men sexually. Larry Bolding had been one of the few exceptions, and that was because he was shit-scared of his wife, political career, and spotless reputation.

Boy, could she blow the whistle on his spotless reputation. Oh yeah, she could *really* make him squirm.

It was days since she'd returned the flowers to Angelo. Now the time was ripe. Picking up the phone, she called him.

Angelo groped for the receiver in his sleep. "Yeah?" he said in a muffled voice.

"Listen, stud," she said. "Don't you think it's about time I taught you how to *really* get it on?"

He was silent, trying to gather his thoughts.

"Last chance, sweetheart," she said mockingly. "So why don't you get your fine ass over here quick, an' I'll show you tricks you ain't *never* gonna forget!"

By the time he was properly awake she'd hung up. It was past midnight. Throwing on some pants and a shirt, he ducked out the back entrance. This was one scene Shifty Fly wasn't going to be following him to.

Chapter 26

Lara paced her living room, smoking agitatedly. It was early; light was just beginning to seep through the darkness. New York was taking shape outside.

Why did I ever become involved? she thought.

Nick was asleep in the bedroom. *Why did it have to be Nick?*

Her hand shook slightly as she dragged on the cigarette, realizing that she didn't want to take it any further. Nick was not responsible for things his father did. Dukey K. Williams was right, and Rio, with her insane plans, all wrong. Much as she had loved Margaret, her sister was dead, and no amount of revenge could bring her back. If Enzio Bassalino *was* the man responsible, then let Dukey deal with him in the way he wanted to.

Oh, God! How had she ever gotten into this? A few hours earlier she and Nick had left Le Club.

"Your place or my hotel?" he'd asked intently.

Lightheaded from too much champagne, she'd replied, "My place."

They'd started to kiss in the car, all over each other like a couple of high-school kids.

"Baby, baby, you make me crazy," he'd said, guiding her hand to the bulge in his pants that lent truth to his statement.

For a moment she'd been overcome with guilt—because she was enjoying his touch, and there was no way she was supposed to enjoy it. But once they reached her apartment her guilt melted away in his arms as he ripped the nine-hundred-dollar black dress off her and made love to her on the floor.

Later he'd carried her into the bedroom, and it had happened one more time before she'd fallen asleep.

Now she was awake, pacing up and down like an agitated cat.

Was it possible to fall in love with someone you were supposed to hate?

"How about some coffee, princess?" Nick

walked into the living room, startling her. He was naked. His body lean, hard, and tanned.

Wrapping his arms around her, he hugged her close and slowly began pushing her negligee off her shoulders, sliding it down her body.

With great anticipation she leaned her head back—all the better to catch his kisses. It had never been this way with anyone before, this pure physical pull. There had always been reasons why she'd gone to bed with men. Hard-hitting, down-to-earth reasons.

With Nick it wasn't like that. Oh, there was a reason, all right. But it didn't matter anymore, it wasn't important.

He lifted her easily and carried her back to the bedroom. "You, lady, are beautiful. I mean *really* beautiful. You know what I'm sayin?"

Yes, she knew what he was saying. She also knew that soon the morning papers would arrive. And how would he feel then?

Beth stayed with the Bassalino children. She felt sick and scared. If anything happened to Anna Maria's baby, it was all her fault, and that didn't bear thinking about.

Frank phoned in the morning. His voice sounded funny. "Pack up and get out of there," he instructed her harshly. "Do it *now*. I don't want to find you around when I get back."

"Is everything all right?" she asked anxiously. "The baby?"

There was silence for a moment, and then Frank's voice cold and loud. "Get the fuck out of my house, you whore. An' don't leave no forwarding address, 'cos if I ever set eyes on you again, I'm gonna kill you." He slammed the phone down.

Beth recoiled in shock. It was over. Whatever it was, it was over. She was free. Now she could go home.

With an unsteady hand she picked up the phone and dialed information, obtaining the number of the hospital.

"I'm inquiring after Mrs. Frank Bassalino. She was admitted early this morning. I'm a relative. Is she doing okay?"

The operator's voice sounded apologetic. "I'm sorry, we cannot give out information over the phone."

Of course not, she thought bitterly. Hurrying to her room, she packed her few things. Minutes later she stepped outside the house. Relief swept over her. Soon she could return to her daughter Chyna and the commune. But first she had to find out about Anna Maria.

A bus dropped her half a block away from the hospital. She was terrified of bumping into Frank, but her fear was overcome by a desperate need to know.

"Mrs. Bassalino died at eight A.M.," a nurse told her. "Complications with the position of the baby, and other things . . ." The nurse trailed off. "Are you a close friend? I think Dr. Rogers might like to speak to you."

"And the baby?"

"Everything possible was done, but I'm afraid . . ."

Beth turned and ran.

The nurse started after her. "Please wait, if you can help us at all—"

Beth kept running. She didn't stop until she reached Grand Central Station, where she bought herself a ticket home.

Before boarding the train she phoned Cass. "I guess it's what you all wanted," she said bitterly. "But how does it help Margaret? It certainly doesn't bring her back, does it?"

Chapter 27

They were making love.

"You're getting better all the time." Rio finally threw a compliment his way. "Maybe I was wrong about you."

Angelo rode the wave. He was in control. Like a car that has been perfectly tuned, he crested each bump and hill and didn't falter.

The Stones mumbled hornily on background stereo. It was early evening, and things had been going successfully all afternoon.

"Let's take a break for food," Rio announced. "I've got a friend who'll bring over anything we want." Rolling away from him, she lifted the phone.

Angelo lay back triumphant. He could go as long as she wanted him to. King Stud.

"Yeah, you can bring Peaches," Rio purred into the receiver. "I'm certain there's plenty to go around. Sure. See you soon. Bye." She flopped back on the bed. "Food's on its way. How about an appetizer, babe?"

Angelo thought about phoning the casino to let them know he wasn't coming in tonight, but what the hell—it would only bring Shifty Fly running to station himself outside, and who needed that?

"I'm ready," he said confidently.

"Great!"

Rio liked popping ammis. Soon she was breaking open another glass vial and forcing it under his nose.

He breathed in deeply, feeling the effect down to his toenails.

"You know, you're not too bad," she murmured, sliding across his body, straddling his neck with her long legs. "But Jesus Christ, your beard is itchy!"

Enzio paced the private room at the hospital, his face a grim mask.

Frank sat in a chair, his head buried in his hands.

Enzio muttered in Italian, occasionally throwing words of contempt in his son's direction.

Dr. Rogers entered the room. He was a weary, bespectacled man with receding hair and a slight build.

Enzio clapped him on the shoulders. "Doctor, we know you did all you could, you mustn't blame yourself."

Dr. Rogers shook Enzio's hand away. "I don't blame myself," he said indignantly. "Not at all, Mr. Bassalino." He turned to glare at Frank. "I'm afraid that poor girl was very badly beaten. The baby had no chance, it was—"

"She fell down the stairs," Frank interrupted, stone-faced. "I told you that before. She fell."

"Mr. Bassalino, your wife's internal injuries were not consistent with falling down stairs. She was beaten, and *that's* what will have to go on the death certificate." His voice was full of barely concealed disgust. "I'm sure there will have to be an inquiry."

Enzio approached the doctor. "Are you a family man, Doc?" he asked, very friendly.

"Yes," the doctor replied shortly.

"Pretty wife? Nice kiddies?"

"I don't see what this has to do—"

"Plenty," Enzio said. "As a family man, you can understand the occasional little tiff. Y'know what I mean—lovers' quarrel, that kind of thing. Happens all the time, don't it, Doc?"

"What has this got to do with anything?" the doctor asked stiffly.

"Well, y'see, my boy—he's a man suffering. Now, you wouldn't wanna make it any worse for him, wouldja, Doc?"

"Mr. Bassalino, I have a duty to perform."

"Sure you do, an' believe me, I'm not trying to stop you. I think you doctors do a wonderful job. And yet you're underpaid. It's shockin'. A crime, really. I mean, here you are workin' your asses off, an' what do you get? Hardly enough to keep your wife looking pretty." Enzio took a beat. "You know what I mean, huh? I'm an old man, but I still appreciate a pretty face." A meaningful pause. "It would be a shame if your wife lost hers." He fumbled in his pocket, producing a wad of bills carelessly held together with a rubber band. "Here's a thousand dollars, Doc, somethin' to help you out."

Dr. Rogers hesitated as Enzio thrust the money toward him.

"Take it," Enzio said, his voice mild. "Keep your wife pretty."

By the time the papers were delivered Nick had fallen back to sleep.

Lara scanned them quickly. In the gossip column of one was the item she had known would be there. The writer—a bitchy woman columnist—had put it together as only a bitch could.

How does glamorous star of the forties, still-frisky April Crawford, do it? Married four times, she is about to take el plunge-o five with handsome, thirtyish Nick Bassalino, a Los Angeles businessman, say those in the know. However, someone should tell Nick, for when last seen, he was boarding a plane for New York with gorgeous, Lara Crichton, a stunning jet-setter of twenty-six. Last report had them dancing cheek-to-cheek, among other things, at New York's chicest discotheque, Le Club.

There was a picture of Lara taken in Acapulco for a *Harpers Bazaar* layout, looking incredible in a one-piece white swimsuit. There was also a picture of April leaving a film premiere. She looked tired.

Oh, well, Lara thought ruefully—good-bye April. The movie star would never stand for Nick making a public fool of her.

What now? Where did it leave her and Nick?

It wasn't fair. She hadn't known it would be like this. She hadn't counted on actually falling in love.

Was one night of incredible sex, love?

Maybe, maybe not. He was so different from

all the other men she'd known. He was masculine and sexual. There was nothing phony about Nick Bassalino. He was just as he was.

Angry at herself, she took the paper in the bedroom and tossed it at him. "You're not going to like this," she said flatly. "And I think it's going to make April mad as hell."

Rio fixed fantastic drinks. Rum, brown sugar, eggs, cream, Benedictine, all mixed together in the blender. When the doorbell rang she told Angelo to stay in bed, she would get it. Naked, except for the stiletto heels she always liked to wear, she marched off.

What with the poppers, the sex, the couple of joints they'd smoked, and the heavy rum drink, he felt pretty tired. Pleasantly so. Christ, she couldn't object to his falling asleep now. There would be no more name-calling; he'd proved himself at last.

He closed his eyes, feeling strange, almost suspended. More than being stoned, it was as if his mind was leaving his body and drifting over to the corner to watch him.

That was funny. That was *really* funny, and he started to laugh. Soon he realized his laugh wasn't coming out of his mouth, it was coming out from all over, his nose, ears, even his ass. The thought only made him laugh more, and the more he laughed the more peculiar sensations overcame him.

He noticed a lot of people crowding into the room. Nice smiling faces that appreciated his laughter.

They all began to take off their clothes, and as they did so the clothes floated around the room in slow motion. Angelo was too exhausted to sit up. He was enjoying himself. He was having such a *great* time.

"Hey, baby." Rio's face swam into focus very close to his. "You remember Hernando and Peaches, don't you, babe? They *both* think you're *reaal* special. They *both* want to meet you."

Her voice saying "meet you" echoed and echoed around the room until it sounded like an Indian mantra.

He nodded. Immediately his head seemed to leave the rest of his body and ricochet up to the ceiling.

Hernando began laying strong hands on him, caressing his sex, taking it in his mouth.

Angelo groaned with pleasure. His penis felt bigger than his body. His body was nothing.

Peaches was exquisite, a fine-boned Slavic face and thick blond hair. She was pushing Hernando away and taking over.

Somewhere Rio's laughter hung heavy in the air.

They turned him over, and Hernando mounted him, and he knew it was a man forcing his way inside, but it didn't matter, it didn't matter at all. In fact, it was fantastic. Peaches was taking him in her mouth at the same time, and he thought he was reaching a pinnacle of eternity, and the actual coming was an explosion that rivaled the atomic bomb.

Pow!! Great mushroom clouds. And he drifted off into the deep sleep he had been waiting for.

Chapter 28

Nick argued impatiently with April Crawford's maid on the telephone. He was lying on Lara's bed. "Now come on, Hattie, I *know* she's there. Tell her again, I *have* to talk to her, it's *very* important."

Hattie lowered her voice. "Mr. Bassalino, it's just no good. She is locked in her room and won't speak to anyone."

"You're sure you told her it's me?"

"*Especially* you she won't talk to."

"Oh, shit, Hattie, you know what she's like. I'll try and get a plane back today. How many bottles has she got in there with her?"

"Mr. Bassalino!" Hattie exclaimed in shocked tones. She had been with April nineteen years and still refused to admit her employer drank.

"Keep an eye on her, Hattie, explain things to her, tell her not to believe everything she reads in the papers. I'll see you tonight."

Lara, hovering outside, marched briskly into the room. "Well," she said, forcing a smile, "that's it, then, is it?"

"What?" he said shortly.

"Running back to Momma's arms, huh? I do hope she'll forgive you for being bad."

He shook his head sadly. "Lara—Lara. I'm surprised at you."

He's surprised at *me!* she thought angrily. Jesus, she'd really been acting like a naïve idiot. Blinded by a great-looking guy with a fantastic body and one night of wild sex. She'd expected he might *want* to stay, but the only thing on his mind was running back to April.

"When are you leaving?" she asked flatly.

"I don't know. I have to call my father."

"Oh, I see. Can't go unless Daddy gives the word. Well, if he says you have to stay another night, shall we enjoy a repeat performance? After all, we're both here, it would be foolish not to take advantage."

"Listen," he said, getting off the bed, still naked. "Don't talk like a cunt, it doesn't suit you. You knew what this was going to be. I never lied to you about me and April. I *love* April Crawford. I'm going to *marry* her."

"You insulting bastard!" She was close to tears. "Just get dressed and get the hell out."

He shrugged. "If it means anything to you, last night was Wonderland."

"And I was Alice, a naïve little girl. Thank you, Nick. You sure made me grow up in a hurry."

He tried to take her in his arms, but she pushed him away.

"When are you coming back to Los Angeles?" he asked.

"Never. Does that make you feel more secure?"

"If we're careful, we can still see each other."

She laughed bitterly. "God, Nick, I don't believe you! In one breath it's how you love April Crawford and you're going to marry her. And in the next it's when will you see me again. Well, let me tell you, Nick Bassalino. You won't—not ever."

He shook his head. "Don't count on it, baby. Just don't count on it."

Golli and Segal arrived at the hospital and escorted Frank home. "Whatever you do, don't leave him," Enzio warned. "Stay with him, keep watchin' him."

Enzio made all the arrangements for the funeral. He had spoken to Anna Maria's family in Sicily. Her mother and sister said they would fly in for the funeral.

Enzio was sick to his stomach. Frank was a bitter disappointment. Beating a pregnant woman was a terrible thing to do. A sin. But thank God it had happened while Enzio himself was in New York and able to deal with matters so there would be no disgrace brought upon the family.

Still, he'd never expected anything like this from Frank, his oldest—and, he'd thought, most dependable—son. God would surely punish him for such a violent and sickening act. Enzio firmly believed in the power of the Almighty for certain things.

What a morning. News of the bombings at Manny's and Barbarellis had reached him. He was sure Bosco Sam was behind it. A show of strength was needed, but Christ, what strength could you show to a bunch of crazy maniacs who walked around in broad daylight blowing up places?

Enzio knew there had to be an answer. There had to be, or the whole Bassalino organization's reputation would be at risk. Who was going to pay protection for no protection?

All morning he'd been trying to reach Angelo in London. It was yet another worry he didn't need. Angelo hadn't shown up at the casino, and somehow he'd managed to disappear without his bodyguard. Out getting laid, of course.

Once more the overseas operator told him there was no reply from Angelo's number. He knew what he would do when he got hold of him. Bring the horny little bastard home for Anna Maria's funeral and keep him home. No more screwing around in London. Angelo's place was with his family, where they could watch him. Maybe he'd put him to work for Frank again.

Finally Nick arrived at the hotel.

"What took you so long?" Enzio snapped. "You shoulda come to the hospital."

Nick was distressed. "I only just heard," he said. "What happened?"

Enzio grimaced sadly. "An accident. She fell down the stairs."

Nick looked incredulous. "Fell down the stairs? How? Where was Frank?"

"He was sleeping. She was pregnant, clumsy on her feet. It was a tragic accident."

"God! I can hardly believe it. Anna Maria was such a sweet kid. . . ."

"And you?" Enzio bellowed. "Where the fuck were you all night? When I need you, no one can find you." He shook his head. "Don't you have no sense, Nick? These are dangerous times."

"I called the hotel soon as I got up," Nick said defensively. "Then I broke my balls rushing over here."

"You broke your balls last night," Enzio commented dryly. "At least it's good you can forget about the old broad you screw in Hollywood. But hey—no time for talk now. You go to your brother's house and stay with him."

"I gotta be getting back to the Coast. Without me things can start—"

"Enough!" Enzio shouted. "I don't understand my children. Your brother loses his wife —*your* sister-in-law. There should be grief, respect. But no, you mumble about getting back to the Coast. What kind of brother are you? Get over to Frank's house an' sit with him. You can plan on stayin' here until after the funeral."

"When's that?"

"Don't question me!" Enzio screamed. "Get out of here." His heart was bouncing around, a sign of overexertion, no doubt.

What had he done to deserve three idiot sons?

Chapter 29

Dukey K. Williams accepted the news of the bombings calmly. He congratulated Leroy.

Later he visited Cass. "I'm leaving the apartment soon," he told her.

The apartment he'd shared with Margaret held too many memories. He had to forget about the past. Remembrances of Margaret were making every day painful. When her death was avenged, he wanted to be ready to move on.

Cass told him about Anna Maria Bassalino and Beth's sudden return to the commune.

"Pull the other two out," he warned harshly.

"*I'm* takin' over now. I'm doin' it my way, and I don't want them around, screwin' things up."

"What are you going to do?" Cass asked, alarmed.

"It's better you don't know," he replied.

Back home he called his manager. "Let's get the show on the road again. I'm gonna be ready to work sooner than you think."

His manager was delighted.

Next he called Leroy. "Why don't we cut the overture an' get down to business? I want this finished. Start with Frank at the funeral for his wife, an' then take care of the house in Miami. No more waiting. Put your plan into action. The money will be ready when you are."

"It's as good as done," Leroy replied. He didn't make idle promises.

Chapter 30

Angelo had trouble forcing his eyes open. With a supreme effort he managed it and blinked several times. His eyes felt crusty and bloodshot. Serious hangover eyes.

For a moment he was completely disoriented, and then he remembered where he was. He was alone on Rio's bed in her apartment. The drapes were closed, and he had no idea if it was night or day.

His body ached, and there was an uncomfortable, unfamiliar feeling about his backside.

"Jesus Christ!" He sat up slowly, gingerly. What the hell had happened to him?

He clearly remembered coming to her apartment, and Rio greeting him. He remembered the fantastic sex scene they'd had, and the ammis, the pot, the drinks. Then everything went blank. One long—how long?—great big blank.

It must have been the drinks. Those thick, creamy rum concoctions Rio had dipped her fingers in and fed him with. They'd knocked him out.

Where was she, anyway?

Unsteadily he got up, aware of the difference in his body, beginning to be much more aware of how it must have happened.

He had to take a piss, and he groped his way into the bathroom.

Scotch-taped to the mirror were six color Polaroids, leaving him in no doubt as to what had happened. In case he was not convinced, Rio had written across the mirror in bright red lipstick: RIGHT ON BABY! I ALWAYS KNEW YOU WERE A FAG.

With mounting horror he stared at the Polaroids. They showed him with a plumpish, dark man and a beautiful blond girl. Only she wasn't a girl, she couldn't be a girl, because in spite of her breasts she also featured a formidable penis.

Angelo had always feared men getting close to him. He hated being touched by them. Even a friendly back pat irritated him. All his life he'd scrupulously avoided any male contact. And now this.

In the pictures he was smiling, laughing. He actually looked like he was *enjoying* it.

Panic overcame him. God Almighty! If anyone *saw* these pictures. If his *father* should see them. Holy shit! It didn't bear thinking about.

Hurriedly he ripped the offending Polaroids off the mirror and tore them into small pieces, flushing the bits down the toilet.

He took a deep breath. With the evidence gone he felt calmer.

What was he worried about anyway? He wasn't gay; half of the women in London could testify to *that.*

It was that bitch Rio's fault. She'd spiked his drink and had her fun. Where was the cow?

He searched the apartment. It was empty. She must have planned the whole sick scene.

Well, he wasn't going to let her get away with it. He would think of *some* form of retaliation to blow her away.

With Nick gone, Lara was keyed up and agitated. Things had worked out as she'd planned, but what if April took Nick back? It wasn't a likely prospect, but what if she did? Then all her scheming and planning would count for nothing—a useless waste of time.

Maybe. Maybe not. Was it useless she'd finally met a man who could make her feel emotions other than how big his bank balance was, or what kind of title he held?

Was it useless she'd fallen in love for the first time ever?

None of it mattered. Whatever the outcome, she didn't care to be involved anymore. And she certainly never wanted to set eyes on Nick Bassalino again.

For insurance she decided to call Prince Alfredo in Rome, or wherever he was, and summon him to fetch her. And then she would phone Cass and tell her it was over.

Decision made, she felt better. Or did she? Nick Bassalino was on her mind, and he wasn't going to be that easy to forget.

Nick went to Frank's house. The children were whiny and noisy.

"Where's the nanny?" he asked.

"Gone," Frank mumbled. He was drinking neat whiskey, hunched in a chair, his eyes bloodshot, his appearance unkempt.

"Jesus, Frank, I'm sorry about everything . . ." Nick trailed off. He'd never been very close to his older brother. When they were kids Frank used to beat the shit out of him. Frank had always been the biggest and the strongest, and he'd never let Nick forget it.

Nick wandered into the room where Golli and Segal were watching television. It was such a depressing house. Old and worn. It was a house that must have looked the same twenty, even thirty years previously. He thought with longing of his own place in Los Angeles. Big and spacious. White and modern. Then he thought of April's rambling mansion, with the lake in the garden and the swimming pool in the living room. California was the only place for him. He enjoyed the climate, the people, the whole relaxed way of living. You could shove New York. Dirty pavements and uptight people. Everyone white-faced and hustling, scurrying around like guests at a rat-fuck.

He went upstairs and placed another call to April. It was the same story. She refused to speak to him. He told Hattie he was delayed, and why. "Be sure to tell her why," he emphasized. April was liable to think he was hanging around to be with Lara.

Thinking of Lara, it had been nice, she was a very lovely lady. But beautiful girls were a plague in Los Angeles. You fell over them everywhere you went. April Crawford was an original, and Nick was confident she would forgive him once he explained there was nothing to it. Lara just happened to be on the same plane—coincidence—it could happen to anyone. And April understood what went on in the gossip columns—pure hokum—nobody ever believed the garbage they printed.

Yes, Nick was sure everything was going to work out fine.

Restlessly he wondered what Lara was doing. Would she hang up if he called her?

He wasn't about to risk finding out. Nope. Best to forget her.

He'd wanted her. He'd had her. End of story.

Christ, it was going to be boring, hanging around the house with Frank.

"Hey, Segal," he yelled downstairs. "How about a game of poker? Any cards around this mausoleum?"

Chapter 31

Mary Ann August woke up in Los Angeles. She couldn't remember much about getting there. After Alio Marcusi had slobbered all over her there had been another visitor, a woman named Claire.

Mary Ann could remember being frightened and telling Claire that when Enzio found out what had happened there would be plenty of trouble. Claire had laughed and called her honey. "Don't worry, honey, Enzio knows all about it. He wants you to come on a little journey with me."

Then Claire had stuck a needle into her arm, making her groggy and docile, and she had dressed and left the hotel with Claire, and there had been a car journey, then an airplane, another car trip, and after that a house, a room, and sleep. Now she was awake.

She got up and took stock of her surroundings. She was in a bedroom, a plain room with olive-green walls and shuttered windows. The shutters wouldn't open, nor would the door.

She peered at herself in a mirror. Her teased hair was sad and straggly, her makeup streaked and faded.

Nothing annoyed Mary Ann more than not looking her best. Searching for her purse, she found it on the floor. Painstakingly she applied fresh makeup and redid her hair. When the two jobs were finished she finally allowed herself to wonder where she was and what was going on.

During her six months with Enzio, Mary Ann had acquired quite a few possessions. Jewelry, clothes, a mink coat—and, of course, her latest acquisition, the full-length chinchilla.

She was thinking of those things now. They were her protection when Enzio finally got tired of her. They would buy her a decent future so she wouldn't have to go back to dancing around naked on a stage for a living. She would kill rather than lose her possessions.

The woman Claire came into the room. She was fortyish and slim, slightly masculine-looking.

"I don't understand," Mary Ann said in her best baby-girl voice. "Where's Enzio? Why does he want me here?"

Claire shrugged. "He figured you needed a change, honey. He knows I have lots of nice friends here in L.A., and he thought you'd enjoy meeting some of them."

"Why didn't he tell me?"

Claire put her arm across Mary Ann's shoulders. "Enzio told me one of your best qualities is that you don't ask a lot of silly questions." She narrowed her eyes. "You're a very pretty girl, but that hairstyle will have to go."

"Enzio likes my hair this way," Mary Ann said stubbornly.

"Get used to it, kitten. Enzio won't be around for a while."

"What about my things? My clothes and jewelry? My fur coats?"

"Don't worry about them," Claire replied easily. "Enzio's having them sent. Be a good girl and cooperate with me—that way everything's gonna turn out okay."

Dumb as she was, Mary Ann was slowly beginning to realize all was not well.

Chapter 32

Shifty Fly saw Angelo safely aboard the big jumbo jet bound for New York. "Don't think it hasn't been fun, Yank," he sneered.

"Listen, man," Angelo said. "Why are you so uptight? I understand you've got your job to do. Only thing is, you're not too good at it."

Shifty Fly glared at him. He'd had a right dressing down from Eddie Ferrantino for allowing Angelo to give him the slip.

"Don't wait around on my account," Angelo continued. "I'm not going anywhere." Leaning back in his seat, he shut his eyes, hoping that by the time he opened them Shifty Fly would be gone. He was.

The day had been a fuck-up. Screaming from every direction. Enzio in New York. Eddie Ferrantino in London. Christ knows what he was supposed to have done. Free, white, and over twenty-one, he'd shacked up with a broad and not told anyone where he was. Terrible thing. A crime.

"Would you like to order a drink, sir?" asked the stewardess. She was pretty in a plastic, groomed sort of way.

Normally he would have imagined screwing her, but his head was so full of other things he hardly noticed her. "Just a Coke," he said.

The two seats beside him were empty, and that pleased him. Later he hoped to be able to lie down and sleep. He needed the rest.

He was apprehensive about seeing his father. Enzio was sure to scream about the way he looked. He hadn't even had time to get his hair trimmed, and it was now as long and thick as a rock star's.

If only he could tell Enzio Bassalino to go fuck himself. But he couldn't. He knew he couldn't. Yet he wasn't sure *why* he couldn't.

As the big jet taxied down the runway Angelo allowed himself to think about Rio. She was some woman, the sort of woman who would stand up to someone like Enzio. One thing about Rio Java. She was an original. She did her own thing.

On the other hand, she was a sadistic bitch. And he wasn't happy about her hyping his drink and involving him in her orgy with her own personal band of perverts. Just whom exactly did she think she was dealing with? He wasn't some schmuck off the street.

He wondered if she would call him. His fast departure for New York had to surprise her. Maybe she would think he was running away. From what? He had nothing to run from. So some guy had made it with him. Big fucking deal. Most men had at least one homosexual experience in their lives.

But when he thought about it his skin began to crawl, his stomach to churn, and a helpless excitement crept through his body. Deep down he knew, although he wouldn't admit it, that it was something he would want to try again.

Lara went to Kennedy Airport to meet Prince Alfredo Masserini. She had called him, told him she needed him, and although he was in the middle of a backgammon tournament in Gstaad, he had promised to fly to her side at once.

She'd decided to meet his plane because she had to keep occupied. Too much thinking was driving her crazy. Nick Bassalino was on her mind with a vengeance, and she didn't know how to forget him.

Prince Alfredo should be able to make her forget.

Sure, a mocking inner voice told her.

At the airport she bumped straight into Nick.

They stared at each other for a moment of complete surprise, then Lara smiled the hurt out of her eyes and extended a hand for her customary European handshake. "Are you returning to Los Angeles?" she asked politely, silently adding, and April?

"No." He shook his head. "My brother's coming in from London. I'm meeting him. What are you doing here?"

"Uh . . . I have friends arriving from Europe." She didn't know why she hadn't said my fiancé, Prince Alfredo Masserini, a Roman prince, not a miserable half-breed Yankee Italian like you.

Twenty-four hours previously they had been in bed together. Now they stood like polite strangers.

Nick peered at his watch. Lara glanced around in the faint hope she might bump into someone else she knew. Someone who could rescue her.

"I guess I'd better check on the plane, see if it's on time," he said. "What flight are you meeting? Give me the number and I'll check that out, too."

She handed him a piece of paper with scribbled details.

"Wait here," he commanded.

As soon as he'd gone she had an insane desire to run. How childish. Wrapping her lynx coat tightly around her, she stood her ground.

He returned shortly. As he approached she noticed women watching him. He was the sort of man you looked at twice. You almost recognized him. Was he an actor, a singer?

"We're meeting the same plane," he announced. "Delayed two hours. Want to go to the airport motel and make crazy, incredible love?" He was smiling slightly. A joke?

She smiled back, coldly. It was a joke she didn't appreciate. "I don't think so."

"Pity." He was in control. "You look very beautiful, like you've done very beautiful things lately."

"How's April?" she asked, briskly changing the subject.

"Great," he lied. "Everything's fine. She understands it was nothing but gossip."

"Only it wasn't," Lara pointed out.

He laughed uneasily. "Yeah, sure. *You* know that and *I* know that, but *we* aren't telling, are we?"

She enjoyed the moment, mocking him with her green eyes. "Aren't we?"

He gripped her firmly by the arm. "I'm buying you a drink," he announced. "We can't just stand here for two hours."

"I'm going back to the city," she said crisply. "I've decided not to wait." Damn Alfredo for making the connection that put him on the same plane as Nick's brother.

"Then you've got time for a drink first."

She wanted to say no, turn and run, get out of his life. But her body begged to stay next to his, and her body wouldn't move.

Taking her arm, he led her to a nearby bar and sat her in a corner booth. She ordered champagne and orange juice. The cocktail waitress looked at her as if she was some kind of nut and then turned her attention to Nick, giving him a suggestive wink.

"I probably won't be able to get back to the Coast for a couple more days," he remarked, "so if you're going to be around, maybe we could—"

"Maybe we could what?" she interrupted icily. "Have a few more secret interludes? A little bit of fun on the side that April won't find out about?"

"You didn't object yesterday."

"Yesterday I had no idea you were going to turn to jelly as soon as you saw our names together in a newspaper."

"I told you the truth about me and April. I haven't been keeping secrets. But that doesn't change the way you turn me on. You *know* you turn me on. And it's the same for you, isn't it?" He took her hand in his and held it tightly. "We've got something goin' together, so don't fight it, lady. Just relax."

How easy to agree with him. Two or three more days of incredible sex. And then what?

"You meet your friends," he was saying, "I'll meet my brother, we'll get that over with, and then later I'll come by your apartment. Nobody has to know, only you and me. This way we're all winners. What do you say?"

Her mind was racing. Nick Bassalino needed to be taught a lesson; he was too sure of himself by far.

She hesitated for only a moment.

"C'mon, Lara," he urged. "Do you have a spare key to your apartment?"

Revenge was sweet. "Yes, as a matter of fact, I do," she said, fumbling in her purse.

Chapter 33

It wasn't fair to blame Beth, Frank reasoned. It wasn't her fault Anna Maria had caught them together. Beth was a good kid, genuinely sweet and concerned. He'd called her a whore. She was probably destroyed. He regretted his phone call telling her to get out. It was stupid. He needed her now, more than ever. The children needed her. How many girls like Beth were there around? Not many, he could vouch for that. The day of the innocent girl was over. They were all hookers and hustlers out for what they could get.

He wanted Beth back. But how was he supposed to find her when he couldn't even remember which employment agency had sent her? He had all of them checked out, but none of them seemed to remember her. At her interview she'd brought references. References he hadn't bothered to check, because he'd liked her at first glance. Now he found himself in the frustrating position of not knowing where she was, or any more about her than that her name was Beth.

He put people in charge of tracking her down, knowing she would have to register with the employment agencies if she wanted another job. Meanwhile, because of his own stupidity, he could only sit and wait. And sitting and waiting meant thinking, and he did not like the thoughts that crowded his head. So he drank, and drinking meant a sweet oblivion that only hit him after a full bottle of Scotch, and being drunk meant he couldn't work.

Enzio gave strict orders to Segal and Golli not to let Frank out of their sight, and to keep him at home. There would be time enough after the funeral to pull Frank back into shape.

In the meantime Enzio took over. First he met with an old friend, Stefano Crown. Stefano was sympathetic; he too was having trouble with new organizations trying to muscle in.

"What's your solution?" Enzio asked.

Stefano Crown shrugged. He was younger than Enzio by fifteen years and still kept complete control of his business empire. "Maybe I give 'em a piece of action, bring some of 'em in," he said.

Enzio spat his disgust on the floor. He'd experienced trouble with Stefano Crown before. The prick was getting soft. "You give 'em some, they want more. You give 'em more, they want it all."

"I run legitimate businesses," Stefano said, stroking his chin. "Last week they blew up two of my supermarkets. Whaddaya think that means? I can't have the ordinary jerks too shit-scared to drag their asses to work in the mornings. Last week thirty-three of my employees quit—*thirty-three*. Word gets around. Soon I'll have 'em all takin' off. Then what'll I do, when there's no one to run the beauty parlors, garages, supermarkets, huh, Enzio, my friend?"

Enzio spat again. All Stefano Crown was concerned about was his legitimate front. Fuck that. Things were so different from the old days.

"You go with 'em, you get no help from me," he said roughly. "I have other plans, better plans."

Stefano shook his head. "I don't want no more trouble. I can't afford it. I'm a man who pays my taxes. A businessman. What does Frank want to do?"

"Frank," Enzio sighed. "Frank has other

things on his mind. You heard about Anna Maria?"

Stefano nodded. "Shockin' tragedy. I feel for you an' the family."

"The funeral's tomorrow. It would be a sign of respect if you attended."

"Of course I'll be there." Stefano extended his hand. "No hard feelings, Enzio?"

"Not at all," Enzio replied evenly. "You do it your way. I do it mine."

Later that day Stefano Crown was shot in the head as he was about to enter an apartment building on Riverside Drive.

"It's a terrible thing when a man can no longer move freely in this city," Enzio said with feeling when he heard.

Alio Marcusi, who was with him at the time, merely nodded.

Chapter 34

"Hey, Angelo baby, you're looking good, *really* good, brother."

Angelo and Nick hugged tightly, genuinely pleased to see each other.

Angelo scratched his beard ruefully. "I guess the old man's going to pop a few buttons when he gets a load of this."

"Well, you are a bit hairy," Nick admitted, "but nothing that good a barber can't take care of."

"Forget it," Angelo said quickly. "I like it. It stays."

"Sure," Nick agreed. "I'm not the one that has to kiss you."

Angelo looked at him sharply. Was there a snide meaning to that remark?

"How was the flight?" Nick asked cheerfully. Bumping into Lara had made him feel great. "Were the stewardesses pretty? Word filters back you were quite a stud in London, but then you always were a horny little bastard."

"You *and* me, bro," Angelo said with a wide grin.

"Hey," Nick reminded him, "remember the time you were shacking up with that hot starlet —the one with the pink Cadillac—and her boyfriend beat the shit out of you?"

"Yeah. How could I forget?"

"Trouble with you is you always got caught. A boyfriend here, a husband there. I'm amazed you survived, asshole!"

Angelo nodded his agreement.

Nick grabbed his arm. "Come on, let's get moving. Enzio's waiting to see you. By the way, take no notice of the armed escort. He's got some crazy idea we make good targets."

Angelo glanced around, observing two men close by. The bodyguard contingent. They followed Angelo and Nick out to the car and got in the front.

Nick took no notice of them, but Angelo couldn't help feeling uncomfortable. He preferred Shifty Fly to a couple of anonymous hoods who looked ready to pump a bullet into anyone.

"So what's goin' on?" Angelo questioned as soon as they were safely in the car. "Why was I dragged back here so fast?"

Nick stared out the window, his expression serious. "You heard about Anna Maria?"

"No, what? Did she have the baby? What is it this time?"

"She's dead," Nick said stonily. "She fell down the stairs at the house."

"What?" Angelo screwed up his face in disbelief. "Fell down the stairs? Are you shittin' me?"

Nick shrugged.

"Hey, did Frank beat up on her? Did that lousy son of a bitch—"

"Shut up." Nick nodded toward the men in the front seat. "We'll talk about it later, in private."

"Jesus!" Angelo exclaimed. "I always liked Anna Maria. What do *you* think really went on?"

"Accidents happen," Nick said noncommittally.

"Yeah, especially around Frank."

Enzio waited at Frank's house. Frank was in the kitchen holding on to a bottle of Scotch, with Golli and Segal close by.

Enzio sat with Alio in the living room. Two of his men were stationed near the back door, another two at the front, and a further couple of men were sitting in separate parked cars outside.

Enzio had decided he couldn't be too careful. Especially now, with Stefano Crown's son bent on revenge. The young blood seemed to think that Enzio was in some way responsible for his father's death.

"Nothing to do with me," Enzio proclaimed, hurt and angry that Georgi Crown should even suspect him. "It was those pieces of shit Stefano wanted to bring in as partners."

Georgi Crown didn't believe him. The Crowns had already opened negotiations with certain black groups, so it would hardly be to their advantage to put a bullet in Stefano Crown.

"I think Georgi Crown needs a rest," Enzio remarked mildly to Alio. "Arrange it. Oh, and also, my friend, please see that a wreath is sent to Stefano's funeral on behalf of myself and my family."

Enzio felt better than he had in years. Life in New York was fast and exhilarating. Miami was boring for a man who had always lived such an active life. Fuck all the Bassalino rivals. Enzio was giving them a taste of their own medicine.

* * *

After her drink with Nick, Lara returned to the city, confused, filled with mixed emotions, and furious with herself for having gotten mixed up in the whole bizarre business. She stopped by Cass's apartment on the way.

"You look lousy," Cass said bluntly.

"I feel worse," Lara replied, fixing herself a drink.

"You heard, then?"

"Heard what?"

Cass brought her up to date on the Frank Bassalino story. "Beth's gone back to the commune. She sounded pretty bad on the phone."

"I wish I'd seen her," Lara replied, wondering why Nick had not mentioned anything about his brother's tragedy.

"I thought we could visit her in a week or two."

"I'd like that. Just tell me when."

Cass nodded. "I don't know what's happening with you and Nick, but I heard from Dukey, and he wants you all out. I think he's right. It's getting too crazy."

Lara wasn't really listening. "I can't be involved anymore," she said, shaking her head.

"I know," Cass agreed. "That's what I just said. Let Dukey do it his way. I'm not sure what he has planned, but whatever it is, I don't think it's safe to be around the Bassalinos. I'm going to contact Rio and tell her."

"She'll probably be arriving in New York at any moment. Nick was meeting his brother Angelo at the airport. He never mentioned a word about his sister-in-law." She laughed bitterly. "I guess it's time for me to return to my former life. You know, fun and games with the jet set. Back to the high life. What do you think, Cass? Will I still fit in?"

"If that's what you want," Cass said evenly. "What happened with Nick Bassalino?"

"Nothing important."

Back at her apartment she studied her face in the bathroom mirror. She seemed to look different, only she didn't know why. Ugly, I look ugly, she thought.

So what good had it all done? Nick appeared to be as resilient as ever. And were they supposed to be glad that Frank Bassalino's wife was dead, along with his unborn child? Carefully she took off her makeup, then just as carefully she applied more. She did it three times before she was satisfied. It kept her from thinking too hard.

Finally she sat in a chair, staring at the front door, waiting for Prince Alfredo.

"You little punk!" Enzio spat, clapping Angelo round the shoulders, kissing him on both cheeks. "You *still* look like a fuckin' communist!"

Angelo joined in the laughter that followed. His father had been saying the same thing to him for years.

"Good to be home, huh?" Enzio said. "It's nice to be with the family in times of trouble."

"Yeah, sure," Angelo agreed halfheartedly. If there was any trouble, he wanted to be long gone.

"You seen Frank yet? I want you to go to him, pay your respects."

Nick went with Angelo to find Frank. Their older brother was sprawled half-asleep in the kitchen.

"Hey, Frank, I'm sorry 'bout things," Angelo mumbled.

Frank grunted.

"Shit, this house is depressing," Angelo muttered in a low aside to Nick. "I hope I'm not supposed to be staying here."

"No, you're at the hotel with Enzio. Anna Maria's mother and sister are arriving later, they're going to be here with Frank an' the kids."

"How long does the old man expect me to hang around?"

"I don't know," Nick said. "The funeral's tomorrow, then Pop has some half-assed idea that we go to Miami for the weekend and see

Rose. He wants us out of the city. Personally, I just want to get back to the Coast."

Angelo scratched his beard. "Hey—you ever wished you were born an orphan?"

Nick laughed. "Every fuckin' day, little brother."

Chapter 35

"You look wonderful," Prince Alfredo Masserini said, kissing Lara on both cheeks. "You have not changed, my darling. You are still the most beautiful woman in the world."

"It hasn't been that long," she commented.

"Too long," he said accusingly. "I have missed you. You have made me look foolish to my friends. All the time they tease me, make jokes. Lara has left, they say." He clicked his tongue disapprovingly. "Your family business has taken you far too much time."

"I'm sorry," she said quietly.

"It is good you are sorry," he replied pompously, loosening his tie and examining his handsome face in a wall mirror for the wearisome signs of travel. "I think now you will not run off like that again."

Jesus, he was full of himself! "No, I won't," she agreed. "I guess it was important at the time, but now . . ." She gestured toward the kitchen. "Are you hungry? I can fix you bacon and eggs."

"Peasant food, my darling. We shall dine out."

"I thought it might be better to stay in." She moved closer to him. "It's been too long."

He was flattered. "You have missed me, Lara?"

"Yes," she lied.

"A lot?"

"More than you'll ever know."

Later Alfredo slept. Lara lay beside him in the big bed. She was wide awake, staring into the darkness.

He did nothing for her. He made her feel empty, used. With Nick it had been so different. So very right.

She wondered if Nick was going to turn up. A quick glance at the bedside clock told her it was late, and she hoped he wouldn't come. It had been stupid of her to give him her key. Such a petty form of revenge.

Prince Alfredo snored offensively. It was very annoying; the noise prevented her from sleeping.

Later she did sleep fitfully, and she had no idea Nick was in the apartment until he switched the bedroom light on and pulled the bedclothes roughly off her and Alfredo. Still half-asleep, she managed a weak "Hello, Nick."

Outraged, Prince Alfredo sat up and furiously demanded, "Who is this person, Lara?" As he spoke he reached for his pure silk underpants.

"You really win the prize," Nick said, shaking his head and staring down at her. "Jesus Christ, you really do."

She didn't try to cover herself, merely returned his stare.

Prince Alfredo flung on a paisley robe. "What do you want?" he asked, his voice becoming high-pitched and out of control.

"There's nothing I want here," Nick replied sourly, throwing her front-door key so it landed on her stomach. "Nothing worth having. Nothing worth paying for."

"Cover yourself," Prince Alfredo shrieked at Lara.

"Hey, bud, no problem. I've seen it all before," Nick said coldly. "Every quivering high-class-hooker inch of it."

"I don't understand," Alfredo whined.

"Nor do I, buddy boy, nor do I." Nick turned to leave, but Prince Alfredo decided it was time to assert his manhood and grabbed him by the sleeve of his jacket.

Nick shook himself free.

"Have you slept with her?" the prince demanded.

Nick's eyes were ice. "Back off, fucker, before I lose my temper," he said roughly.

Alfredo grabbed him again. "You will answer my question!"

With one easy movement Nick smashed his knee into the prince's groin. At the same time his fist connected with the royal nose. Alfredo was out for the count.

Lara didn't move.

Nick paused for a moment and glanced at her. He went to say something, thought better of it, and abruptly left.

Frank couldn't sleep. He refused to go to bed; all he wanted to do was sit in a chair in the kitchen guzzling from a bottle of Scotch and occasionally dozing off. It had been that way ever since the accident.

Nobody said anything. They left him alone. Enzio had attempted several times to engage him in conversation about business activities, but after a while he'd given up. "When the funeral is over you'll pull yourself together," he'd muttered. "A few days in Miami. You'll spend time with your mother, Rose. It'll do you good."

Like hell he'd go to Miami. He wasn't going anywhere until they found Beth.

Anna Maria's mother and sister arrived. It was fortunate they did not speak English. After a short greeting they left Frank alone, and that was the way he wanted it. Alone with his thoughts, his plans for the future. Family business did not enter his mind; let Enzio worry about all that crap.

He thought he might take a vacation, go to Hawaii or Acapulco. Somewhere far away where he could be alone with Beth.

After the funeral he would find her, he had no doubt of that.

Nick left Lara's apartment in a fury. How could she have screwed him like that? What kind of a woman was she?

He went to the best whorehouse in New York. He needed *something* to calm him down.

They put out the red carpet for him. Nick Bassalino. Enzio's son. Frank's brother. It was almost like a visit from royalty.

The madam, a Scandinavian lady with big boobs and a girlish face, offered to serve him personally. He declined her invitation and cho[illegible] a sour-faced redhead instead. The woman kept their encounter on the impersonal level he wished for. It was not satisfactory.

Afterward he was so pissed off he got good and drunk on straight brandy.

Finally he went back to his hotel, booked a call to April Crawford in Los Angeles for early morning, and slept fitfully.

The call came through while he was still asleep. He held the phone to his ear and listened to the long-distance ringing while he tried to open his eyes. His mouth felt like lead shit.

Faithful Hattie told the operator Miss Crawford was not at home, so he spoke to Hattie.

"Hey, Hat, what's happening? She's not *still* mad, is she?"

"Haven't you heard, Mr. Bassalino?" Hattie sounded embarrassed.

"Heard what?"

"Miss Crawford and Mr. Albert were married yesterday."

He was silent.

"Mr. Bassalino, are you there?" Hattie asked in a worried voice. "I *told* Miss Crawford she should have let you know."

Nick put the phone down, his face tense. He called the desk and had them send up the newspapers, and there it was in black and white. Proof positive.

LAS VEGAS. MONDAY.

April Crawford and Sammy Albert

April Crawford took husband number five today in a quiet ceremony in the garden of Stanley Graham's Hi-Style Hotel. Sammy Albert, thirty-year-old star of Road Job, Tiger, *and* Prince California, *was the lucky man. His only comment on the twenty-year age difference was, "April is a real lady, a class act. Her age is of no interest to me."*

Nick threw the paper on the floor in disgust. Jesus Christ, but April was stupid. Any woman who would marry a juvenile super-stud like Sammy Albert was out of her fucking mind. She must have done it in a fit of jealous rage; that was the only feasible explanation.

He couldn't believe it. April and Sammy! It was a bad joke.

He was angry, and yet at the same time, in a strange way, he was relieved. Now that he didn't have to answer to April he was free.

And now that he was free maybe he could do something about Lara.

Chapter 36

Leroy Jesus Bauls did not smoke; it was bad for your health, and Leroy never did anything that was bad for his health.

He was still at a loss to explain his behavior at Manny's. What a stupid, fucked-up thing to have done, getting the old lady and the kid out. So it had turned out all right, and that was fortunate. But it had meant taking unnecessary risks, and that was not his bag.

Never again, he vowed. If anyone got in his way in the future, it was their problem.

Once again he wore his errand-boy clothes as he sat in the parked van a block away from the entrance to the cemetery. A lesson Leroy had learned early in life was that a black in New York could hang around anywhere as long as he dressed the part. Wear something sharp, and stand on a street corner, and the cops were there in no time, hustling you, moving you on. Stand there like a janitor holding a broom, and you were on your own; nobody noticed you.

Leroy was parked in a prime position, the perfect spot to watch the limousines as they arrived in a long, dark, sober parade. His shades were fitted with special telescopic lenses, so recognizing the mourners was no problem.

He noted that Enzio Bassalino was taking no chances. Enzio was surrounded by his men, old cockers in shiny suits with stealthy, darting hands.

Nick and Angelo Bassalino arrived in a car together. They, too, were surrounded by protection as they waited on the sidewalk for Anna Maria's mother and sister, who came in the next car with the children.

Leroy sat perfectly still, watching, noting every detail.

He was good at waiting. The first words he could remember being spoken to him when he was a kid were "You sit still and wait. Y'hear me? Just wait." His mother repeated that phrase to him every day when she left him outside hotel rooms. It was only when he was big enough to peek through keyholes that he realized why she wanted him to wait.

Frank Bassalino arrived. Leroy's knuckles slowly whitened as he gripped the steering wheel hard. It was the only sign he gave that Frank was the one he'd been waiting for.

Eventually they all disappeared into the cemetery grounds, the family, relatives, and friends.

A group of four men remained outside. They split into twos and stayed each side of the gates, their eyes ever-watchful.

Leroy did not move for ten minutes, then he got out of the van, opened up the back, and took out a giant wreath. Slowly he carried it down the street toward the cemetery.

One of the men blocked his path at the gate. "Yeah? Whatcha want?"

"Special delivery for the Bassalino funeral," Leroy said solemnly.

"Leave it here."

"Sure." He deposited the wreath on the ground, fumbling in his pocket for the receipt book. "Sign here, please."

The man scrawled an illegible signature.

Leroy hesitated, as if waiting for a tip. "You want I should take it through?" he asked. "I was given instructions it had to be left graveside."

"Just leave it where it is."

Leroy shrugged. "It's your funeral," he muttered under his breath as he walked back to the van.

Exactly six minutes later the four men standing by the cemetery gates were blown to pieces.

Leroy, now parked three blocks away, heard the explosion clearly. He waited for half a minute and then walked back to view the chaos, carrying a brown-paper parcel.

Police sirens screamed through the air. A crowd was gathering.

Leroy found it was easy to place his package on the front seat of Frank Bassalino's limousine. The chauffeur had left the car and was among the crowd by the cemetery gates. The line of parked limousines was deserted. Leroy realized if he'd so desired he could have left a package in each car. But that wasn't the way Dukey K. Williams wanted it.

Within minutes Enzio and his sons came rushing out. There was much confusion, women were weeping and screaming, and the crowd was growing by the minute.

Leroy strolled casually off, the first part of his job successfully accomplished.

Chapter 37

Angelo could feel the fear in his stomach, a tight, burning knot of pure terror.

They had been standing by the grave when they heard the explosion. Instinctively he dropped to the ground, burying his head in his hands.

Jesus, what a fucking noise! What was he doing here anyway, in this maniac city, when he should be safely in London?

Nick dragged him up. "Stay easy," he warned. "Don't panic. Act like a man, for crissake."

Enzio was already sending people to find out what was going on.

Within minutes they were back with the bad news. A bomb.

Immediately Enzio took command. "Go to the cars. Keep alert. Stay in groups. Golli, Segal, hold on to Frank. Nick, look after Angelo."

Frank appeared to be unaffected by the explosion. He had started the day drunk, and with the help of a flask in his back pocket, he planned to finish the day drunk.

"Go straight to the airport," Enzio instructed. "*Don't* stop by Frank's house or the hotel."

No one argued. With bombs going off around them a weekend in Miami seemed like a good idea.

"I'll take Frank with me," Nick said.

"No, you stay with Angelo," Enzio insisted, noticing how white-faced and shaken his younger son was. "Golli an' Segal will take care of Frank."

Nick didn't argue. All he wanted was to get the fuck out of there before the cops arrived. Let Enzio deal with the police—he was the one with enough connections to wire a building.

They bundled into the cars. Angelo slumped back on his seat. "Those guys," he mumbled. "Those poor goddamn guys. . . ."

"Why don't you thank your skinny balls it wasn't you?" Nick said grimly. "It was probably meant to be."

"Me?" Angelo was incredulous. "Why me?"

"You, me, Frank. What difference? We're all Bassalinos."

Angelo nodded helplessly. Yes, they were all Bassalinos, and that meant anyone warring with Enzio automatically included his three sons.

"Who do you think did—"

"Listen kid, I don't want to talk," Nick interrupted. "Sit back and relax, turn on or something, but leave me alone. I've got some thinkin' to do." He closed his eyes. All day long he'd been trying to get his thoughts straight, and it wasn't easy. For someone who didn't drink he had one bitch of a hangover. The business with Lara had really turned him over. Jesus, she'd planned it, *wanted* him to find her in bed with that Italian piece of shit.

She was a prize bitch.

And yet . . .

He hoped he'd damaged the guy.

He wished he'd damaged her.

And as for April Crawford—she and Sammy Albert would soon be yesterday's news. If he *really* thought about it, they deserved each other.

Lara Crichton was something else. When the

trouble was over and he could concentrate, he was going to have to do something about her. She was too special to let go.

"I don't know why I couldn't have stayed in London," Angelo complained, interrupting his brother's thoughts.

Before Nick could reply they both heard the explosion. It came from behind.

The car with Frank in it was behind.

Chapter 38

Prince Alfredo Masserini had suffered a broken nose. "I will sue that man for every dollar he has," he ranted from his private hospital bed, his perfect Roman nose encased in a plaster cast.

"You don't know who he is," Lara remarked calmly.

Prince Alfredo swore hotly in Italian, then said, "Lara, you are being a very stupid girl. I thought perhaps there was a future for us together, but now . . ." He shrugged, trailing off.

Lara got up from the chair beside the bed and

nodded. "You're right, Alfredo. You really are." She walked toward the door. She'd had enough of him and his whining. News of April Crawford's surprise marriage to Sammy Albert was all over the papers. What was Nick doing? Thinking? Was he destroyed?

"Where are you going?" Alfredo demanded imperiously.

She shook her head. "Paris, maybe. The Bahamas.I don't know."

"You wait here a few days," he said, condescendingly. "I will forgive you. We go somewhere together."

"Ah, but I don't want to be forgiven," she replied, her green eyes bright. "I'm not a child, Alfredo. The truth is, I'm sorry about your nose. I'm sorry about everything. It's just best we don't see each other again."

"Lara!" He was shocked. "What do you mean? I have waited these last weeks, I have made certain plans for us. My mother, she looks forward to meeting you. We ski first, then on to Rome, where I will present you to my family."

"No," she said firmly. "It's over." She left the room, hardly listening as he burst into a stream of angry Italian.

As she walked down the corridor she felt completely blank. Nothing mattered, nothing at all. She was very tired, and the only thought that appealed to her was to climb into bed, bury herself beneath the covers, and sleep. Maybe for days.

She wished the impossible. She wished she had Margaret to talk things over with.

Outside she climbed into her chauffeured car and closed her eyes. "My apartment," she instructed the driver.

"The city's goin' mad," he informed her. "There's hoodlums runnin' wild blowin' each other up. It ain't safe drivin' no more."

Lara wasn't really listening. She was already drifting into sleep.

There was no body to identify. No body to bury. Frank Bassalino had been blown into a thousand little pieces. Two people innocently standing near the car were killed; many more were injured as the blast blew out all the windows in nearby office buildings and shards of glass came showering down.

Nick didn't hang around. He took it all in at a glance and knew Frank had no chance. Thinking quickly, he hauled Angelo out of their own car and, holding him tightly by the arm, marched him away from the wreckage.

Angelo was too shaken to talk. Nick moved fast; they were three blocks away when several police cars zoomed past.

When Nick was sure they weren't being followed he hailed a cab and told the driver to get them to the airport as speedily as possible.

"Somebody's going to get his balls sledgehammered for this," he said at last. "And *I* am gonna do it. *I'm* gonna cut his fuckin' balls off and string them up for salami."

Angelo was a nervous wreck. "Who did it?" he asked, trying to keep the fear out of his voice.

"We'll find out," Nick replied grimly. "We always find out. Nobody gets away with killing a Bassalino."

"You're beginning to sound like Enzio."

"I hope so, little brother. I really hope so."

Rio Java flew into New York and saw the headlines.

She went straight to Cass's apartment. Dukey was already there. "Did you arrange it?" she asked.

He made a vague gesture. "Maybe I did, an' maybe I didn't. We're not the only ones who want to see the Bassalinos go down."

"Well, don't touch Angelo—he's mine. Understand, brother?"

"Sure," he agreed. "If you get to him first."

"I don't have to get to him. I just want to destroy him. Isn't that supposed to be the plan?"

Dukey nodded. "That was before. Things are different now."

"What do you mean, things are different now?"

"Let's just call it a little racial problem and leave it at that."

"Racial problem my ass!" she exploded.

"Listen," he said angrily. "You had your chance, an' you blew it. Now it's my turn."

"Oh," she said coldly, "you mean I'm supposed to drop everything on account of what *you* say."

"Clever girl."

"Don't call *me* girl, asshole."

"Beth and Lara are already out," Cass interrupted quickly, looking to avoid a fight. "I think Dukey's right, Rio."

Rio turned on her. "Oh, do you? Well, fuck you, too."

Dukey's eyes were hard and cold. "Shame you're not black."

"I'm multicolored. It's more fun."

"You're just pissed you can't play any more of your mind games."

"I can do what I like, Dukey. And don't you forget it."

He nodded in agreement. "Sure, babe. Only don't do it near the Bassalinos, 'cos your long, skinny, multicolored ass gonna get blown all the way to hell an' back. Okay, babe?"

Chapter 39

Mary Ann August smiled at Claire, and Claire said, "Honey, you've really surprised me. Things are working out fine. Mr. Forbes was very pleased today, and for Mr. Forbes to be pleased—well, that's really a compliment."

"He promised he'll be back soon," Mary Ann said, stretching her arms above her head so the short, white nightgown she wore pulled up, exposing a fine matting of pale-coffee-colored pubic hair.

Claire's eyes wandered down to take a peek.

No trouble with this one. Some girls were born to be whores.

Mary Ann flopped back on the bed, parting her thighs. "Gee, Claire, I wish I could take a walk," she said innocently. "I'm really cheesed about being shut in all the time. I need fresh air."

"Next week," Claire promised.

Mary Ann pouted. "You *can* trust me, I'm not going to run off. I *like* it here. I like you. . . ." She threw her captor a long, lingering look.

Claire moved nearer to the bed. "You're a smart girl. No trouble. A girl like you can make a lot of money if you want to. Now that we've fixed your hair you look so pretty."

Mary Ann smiled. "Enzio wouldn't like it this way."

Claire sat down on the bed and casually ran her fingers up Mary Ann's leg, heading toward the fuzz. "Enzio's not going to have to like it, is he?"

Mary Ann giggled, spreading her legs apart. "Are you a dyke, Claire?" she asked, licking her lips.

The pressure of Claire's fingers hardened. "I've seen too many potbellies and limp hard-ons to be anything else." A pause. "Have you ever tried it?"

Mary Ann giggled again. "Mr. Forbes couldn't make me come. I told him a little head would do the trick, but Mr. Forbes said that was *my* job."

Claire bent down slowly, her eyes bright. "Mr. Forbes must be screwy in the mind."

Mary Ann sighed and lay back, ready to enjoy the ministrations of Claire.

Five minutes passed. Soon Claire was thoroughly engrossed in the task at hand.

Carefully Mary Ann reached under the bed and got a firm grip on the chair leg she'd hidden there earlier. She then raised her upper body until she could see the top of Claire's close-cropped head. She moaned, causing Claire to increase her efforts. Then slowly, so as not to disturb anything, she raised the chair leg and smashed it down heavily on Claire's head. Once, twice, three times.

There was blood as Claire slumped to the floor, and Mary Ann was sorry about that. But she certainly had no intention of being locked up and forced into the life of a prostitute. Oh, no. Oh, dear me, no. Not Mary Ann August. Not after she had worked hard and put up with Enzio Bassalino for all those months. She had jewelry, clothes, and two fur coats. She had possessions worth money—enough money that, if she sold them, she could go back to the small town in Texas she hailed from and buy herself a nice little business. A boutique, perhaps, or maybe a beauty parlor. She had known her time with Enzio was not a permanent thing and had planned accordingly.

Dressing hurriedly, she took money and keys from Claire's pocketbook.

Mary Ann August had possessions—and son of a bitch, she was going to get them.

Chapter
40

By the next day the house in Miami was buzzing with activity. There was a meeting in progress.

Enzio sat behind his desk, his eyes red-rimmed, shoulders slumping heavily. Beside him stood Nick, doing most of the talking, words coming hard and fast.

Enzio appeared to have aged ten years as he listened to his middle son, occasionally nodding to let the room crowded with men know he was in agreement with everything Nick said.

Angelo hunched in a chair nearby. He was scared, and it showed. His face was white, and his hand was unsteady as he gulped mouthfuls of Scotch from a large tumbler. What he really needed was to get good and truly stoned. A few joints would calm him down and stop the shaking. Only he couldn't turn on in front of Enzio. His father didn't approve of drugs.

Nick was surprisingly cool as he issued instructions. He wanted information, and he wanted it fast. He offered a ten-thousand-dollar reward for the right information.

When the meeting was over the men dispersed.

"Rose," Enzio mumbled. "For Christ's sake, somebody's got to tell her."

Angelo buried himself in his drink. His mother scared the shit out of him. She always had. Frank was her favorite, and Nick seemed to make out okay, but to Angelo she'd always been crazy Rose.

"I'll tell her," said Nick, saving Angelo any excuses. He could communicate with his mother if she was in a good mood. Sometimes he was even able to get her to summon up a faint smile from her otherwise dead face. "I'll go see her now."

Rose sat in her usual chair by the window, gazing out.

Nick crept up behind her and squeezed her shoulders. "Ciao, Mama." He was shocked at how thin she seemed.

Rose looked up at him without a flicker of surprise, nodding slightly, even though it was over a year since she'd seen him.

"I'm sorry it's been so long, Mama," he said. "But you know how it is. I've been busy out on the Coast. You look great, you really do."

Nick could remember his mother before she had locked herself away. He recalled her startling beauty, vivacious personality, and the way she used to make friends so easily.

He also remembered the night it all happened. He was sixteen and out on a date. When he'd returned home Alio met him at the door and told him his mother was sick. "You're to stay at my place tonight," Alio had said. "Angelo and the nanny are already there." Alio hadn't even let him into the house to get his toothbrush.

For two weeks he wasn't allowed home, and when he finally was, he found his mother had locked herself away, refusing to speak to any of them. She kept up her silence for several years, until Enzio moved them all to the Miami mansion. There she staked out her room overlooking the pool and never emerged, although she did deign to speak to her sons occasionally.

"Frank's dead," Nick blurted out. "It was an . . . accident."

Rose spun around and stared at him. She still had the most magnificent eyes he'd ever seen. They could burn a hole in you, they were so deep and bright. Her eyes spoke for her; they begged him to tell her more.

"Uh . . . I don't know much. He was in a limo. There was an explosion. . . ." He put his arms around his mother. What more could he say?

"Enzio," she muttered accusingly. *"Basta!"*

And then there was silence.

Chapter 41

"Strike before they strike back." Those were the orders Leroy Jesus Bauls received from Dukey K. Williams. Which was why he was now on the road to Miami. It was a long drive, but it would have been too dangerous to fly with the equipment he needed. All the security at airports today, luggage being searched and people being frisked. He wouldn't have gotten anywhere near a plane.

His black Mercedes roared down the highway at a steady pace. Leroy was completely at ease, his mind clear and able to deal with the job ahead.

He'd thoroughly inspected Enzio Bassalino's mansion a few days previously, before the family had arrived. Enzio was in New York, so the grounds had not been as closely guarded. With no family present it had been a relatively simple matter to gain access to the house posing as a telephone engineer. The oldest trick in the world, but once the telephone went dead it always worked. Cut the lines, wait twenty minutes, then appear. "Telephone engineer, fault reported on your line." Guards check the phone, check his phony credentials, and nod agreement that he can come in. At first someone follows him everywhere, but then they get bored and he's on his own. Ready to do whatever he wants.

He'd set the house up exactly as he wanted it. Only the finishing touches were needed. He was well aware of the guards at the gates, the alarm systems, the dogs.

It was an exciting job, a challenge, and Leroy looked forward to challenges.

Mary Ann August purchased a long black wig. It covered her blondness nicely. Next she bought jeans, a T-shirt, a man's shirt, and tinted glasses. Hurrying to the ladies' room, she washed off her makeup and put on the new clothes. When she emerged she looked like a different girl.

A cab took her to the airport, where she got herself a ticket for Miami.

She was extremely jumpy. There had been a lot of money in Claire's purse, and she was sure that someone would come after her if just for that. But they wouldn't find her—she didn't even recognize herself in the mirror.

After buying a selection of magazines she boarded the plane.

Nick was in charge. The old man had gone to pieces, his age suddenly and surprisingly catching up with him.

Angelo sat around, restless and manic, until Nick finally got one of the boys to fix him up with a couple of joints to calm him down.

After the meeting Nick phoned Los Angeles to check on business. Everything seemed okay. He had good people working in L.A. Men he could trust.

He kept on thinking about Lara. April was a distant memory. So he wasn't going to be Mr. April Crawford. Big deal. So what?

The old man was resting, and Angelo was playing cards out by the pool.

Nick called the gate. No problems. He'd put an extra man out there. Now there were three of them on constant alert, and no one was allowed through unless they got his personal okay.

The Bassalino family was under fire, and Nick was taking no risks.

Picking up the phone, he dialed Lara in New York. He couldn't help himself.

She took her time answering.

"Listen, lady. You're lucky I didn't kill the sonofabitch," he said threateningly. She didn't answer, so he added, "If I catch anybody in bed with you again their number is up. Do you understand what I'm sayin'?"

"You broke his nose," she said quietly.

"Yeah? That's a shame."

"It's not a joke. He'll probably sue you."

"I'm shakin' in my boots."

"Why are you calling me?"

"I wanted to."

She was ridiculously pleased to hear from him, and yet she couldn't just give in and fall into his arms because April had married Sammy and Nick was now on the loose.

"I'm in Miami," he said. "I want you to go straight to the airport an' catch the next plane here. We have a lot of talking to do."

Breathlessly she said, "Are you crazy?"

"Yeah, I'm crazy," he replied recklessly. "Crazy about you. I need you here, Lara. It's got nothing to do with April and Sammy. I want you. Don't let me down, baby."

"I can't, Nick, I—"

"Don't fight it, sweetheart. We belong together, and you know it. I'll have a man at the airport to meet you—he'll bring you straight to the house."

She felt lightheaded. He needed her. He wanted her. "Okay," she whispered. What the hell, she'd never made a spontaneous decision in her life. Now was the time to take a risk and do something just for Lara.

Before she changed her mind she began throwing things into a suitcase, humming softly to herself, until suddenly Cass's words hit her. Words she hadn't really listened to before were now very clear in her head.

"Let Dukey do it his way. I'm not sure what he has planned, but whatever it is, I don't think it's safe to be around the Bassalinos."

She experienced a moment of panic. Quickly she phoned Cass. "What did you mean when you said it's not safe to be around the Bassalinos?" she asked urgently. "What does Dukey plan to do?"

"I don't know," Cass replied. "I guess he's going to finish off—"

"Finish off *what?*"

"I don't know."

Slamming the phone down, she tried to reach Dukey. There was no reply at his apartment.

Oh, God! She had to get to Nick, tell him the truth, and warn him.

Finishing her packing, she called down to the doorman to find her a cab.

Miami was her next stop. And as quickly as possible. There was no other way of warning him.

Sitting in her room, Rose Bassalino brooded. She had no tears left to cry for her oldest son. Her tears had all been shed many years before.

It was Enzio's fault, of course. Everything was always Enzio's fault. *Basta!* Bastard! Big man with a big cock.

He had taken Frank away because he knew Frank was her favorite.

If she closed her eyes, she could picture in vivid detail that night so many years ago when Enzio and his men had sliced Charles Cardwell to death in front of her. Like a piece of beef they had sliced and carved and hacked.

Animals!

And all the while Enzio had held her, his hands on her breasts, his body stiffening with excitement.

Rose stifled a scream as the memories came crowding back. She stared out of her window. The pool was still there, the grass, the trees. She had trained her mind to go blank, shut out everything, concentrate on the scenery. Over the years she had even managed to ignore Enzio's succession of whores.

Today it didn't work. Today the sun-drenched garden and bountiful greenery did nothing to calm her.

Rose Bassalino was not crazy. She was as sane as anyone. But to hang on to her sanity she had shut herself away, and now she could feel the fury building in her body, a fury giving her new strength.

For her children's sake she had remained in her room for years. It spared them the agony of what she might do if she ever returned to the real world.

Now it didn't matter. Frank was gone. And it was Enzio's fault.

Rose stood up and stepped away from the window.

She knew what she had to do. Her mind was clear for the first time in seventeen years.

Chapter 42

"Angelo—it's the telephone for you." Alio strolled out to the pool to tell him.

"For me?"

"Yeah—a woman." Alio was not interested.

Angelo put down his cards. Nobody knew where he was. He picked up the phone beside the pool.

"You little prick," a familiar voice said. "Running away ain't gonna get you but *nowhere*, baby!"

He recognized her voice immediately. It wasn't difficult. "Rio. How did you find me?"

"I *smelt* you out, baby." She laughed. "We still friends?"

He relaxed. "Yeah, but I want to talk to you."

"To me." She paused. "*And* my friends?"

"Listen, that was strictly a one-time scene."

"Sure, sure. And you hated it—right?"

Once again he experienced the excitement he'd known that time in her apartment. "I don't go that route," he said slowly.

"Oh, *come on*," she replied mockingly. "This is *me* you're talking to. And I am right here at the Fontainebleau with two divine *new* friends who are *aching* to meet you. Shall we come to you, or will you sashay your *nice, tight* ass over here?"

His throat was dry and constricted. "I can't see you today," he said weakly. Nick had given strict instructions that nobody was to leave the house.

Her voice purred raunchily over the phone. "But Angelo, baby. I am naked and horny, and I *never* take no for an answer. My friends are naked and horny and very, *very* willing to do *anything* your little heart desires. They are also *very* impressed with your advance publicity. I showed them the pictures—pictures I'm sure you wouldn't want Daddy to see. So come on over *now*, baby."

He had wanted to go, and now he had to go. The only problem was getting out.

* * *

The only problem was getting in.

More than anyone, Mary Ann August realized how heavily guarded the Bassalino mansion was. She had lived there all those months, and she knew Enzio's stringent methods for keeping strangers out.

However, she was banking on the fact that she wasn't a stranger. She was Enzio's girlfriend, his mistress, and as far as everyone was concerned, she had gone to New York with him just over a week before. And it was perfectly logical that she'd come back with him. She didn't think Enzio would have bothered to announce the fact he was sending her away. He'd obviously told Alio, had him do his dirty work, but apart from that—well, she was sure she knew him well enough to know he kept things to himself.

Mary Ann August had a plan. It was risky. But with luck and guards she knew on the gate, things might just work out.

"I'm going to the airport," Nick said.

"Hey, I'll go with you." Angelo saw a way out. Drive to the airport with his brother and then get conveniently lost.

"No." Nick shook his head. "You stay here and take over from me. There's no way of knowing what their next move is."

Angelo hesitated. He didn't want to argue

with Nick, but then again he was desperate to get out.

Nick was already on his way to the door. Angelo decided to hang back. It would probably be simpler to split when Nick wasn't there anyway.

"Sure, I'll take care of everything," he said. "You can depend on me."

Chapter 43

Enzio awoke around five. His bedroom overlooked the pool, and when he got up he walked over to the window and gazed out for a while.

He felt old and tired. Feelings he wasn't used to. Age was a son of a bitch. In two months' time he would be seventy years old. Frank was only thirty-six, and the bastards had murdered him—a man in his prime, a Bassalino.

Enzio swore to himself, a slow murmuring of never-ending curses. A prayer of obscenities.

He would have liked to have gone to Rose; she was the only one who could possibly understand the pain he was going through.

But it was impossible. Rose had sworn never to talk to him again, and he knew his wife. She would try and punish him for the rest of his days. Not that he let it bother him. She was lucky he hadn't thrown her out.

Perhaps he should visit the girl he'd imported from New York—the one Kosta Gennas had brought him—what was her name? Mabel? No, Miriam. That was it, Miriam. She had been sent to the house and installed in the usual room, but so far he'd not visited her.

"Filth!" With a sudden show of anger he spat on the floor. They were all filth, these women he could buy. Besides, he could summon no sexual interest. At his age it was becoming more difficult.

He lay once again on his bed. Maybe he would sleep some more; perhaps he would feel better in a while.

Images of Frank as a child kept flashing before him. They'd called him Frankie, and the kid was a tough little monkey. He remembered the day Frankie lost his first tooth. The day he learned to swim. The time at school he beat up a boy twice his size. Oh, that had made Enzio so proud! When Frankie was thirteen he'd taken him to his first girl—an eighteen-year-old hooker. Frankie had performed like a man. From that day on they'd called him Frank.

Enzio chuckled, although his eyes were filled with tears.

The door to his room opened quietly. For a moment he couldn't quite make out who it was standing there. Then he recognized Mary Ann August, with her teased blond hair, small red bikini, long legs, and large breasts.

"Hi, baby-sweetie-pie," she said, smiling nicely.

He grunted, struggling to sit up. Hadn't he sent her away? Hadn't Alio dealt with her?

Mary Ann swayed toward the bed. "How's mommy's big bad man?" she cooed, at the same time undoing the tie on her bikini top, allowing her breasts to tumble out.

Enzio's mind was muddled. Alio must have screwed up. Anyway, so what? Mary Ann August was just what he needed now. She knew what he liked, his fads and fancies.

Suddenly he wasn't an old man of nearly seventy, he was a Bassalino, a stud.

Reaching the bed, she leaned over him, her breasts dangling tantalizingly over his face. He opened his mouth and attempted to cram in an obliging nipple.

She giggled and began fiddling with his clothes.

He closed his eyes and sighed as he felt the erection beginning.

His mouth was full of her when she shot him precisely and silently straight through the heart.

Chapter 44

Angelo left the house soon after Nick. It was easy. Just walk out, climb into his old souped-up black Mustang, drive to the gates, wave at the guards as they let him through. Easy. After all, he was a Bassalino, too, so who dared to stop him?

He switched on the radio. Bobby Womack. Loud and clear. Great. He felt good, a little high, just enough. Frank's death had completely unnerved him. A fucking bomb right in the middle of New York—that was one hell of a way to go. But he couldn't pretend he was heartbroken. Okay. Sure. So Frank was his brother. But he'd always been a mean bastard. There had never been any love lost between the two of them.

The thought of seeing Rio again filled him with elation. *She* was sending for *him*. *He* wasn't phoning *her*, groveling for a chance to prove himself. She'd tracked *him* down and flown to Miami especially to see him.

He put his foot down a little harder on the accelerator. Mustn't keep her waiting. Rio was not a woman to keep waiting.

He turned the radio louder. The disc jockey was talking in rhyming slang, jazzing his audience up for James Brown. The Man. Sexy sexy sexy.

Angelo couldn't help laughing aloud. James Brown reminded him of his first scene with Rio. "Sex Machine" had been the record then. He turned the radio up full volume so the sound flooded all around him in a deafening roar. Revving the engine, he shoved his foot down to the floor.

"Rio, baby," he shouted. "Here I come!"

He failed to see the red light ahead. The car plunged through the junction and smashed straight into the side of a massive oil tanker.

Angelo was killed instantly, but on the car radio James Brown sang on. . . .

Chapter 45

"Hey." Nick gripped her by the arms and stared intently into her green eyes.

Lara smiled. "You came to the airport yourself."

"I couldn't wait any longer. Has anyone ever told you you're the most beautiful woman in the world?"

"I love you, Nick," she said simply. "That's why I came."

"Hey, here's a lady who says it like it is." He kissed her. "I love you, too, princess. You got any suitcases?"

She nodded. "One."

He took her hand, holding it tightly as they walked through the terminal to wait for her luggage.

"Listen to me," he said. "There's so many things I want to tell you."

"There's plenty I *have* to tell you, too, Nick."

"Okay. So we have all the time in the world, don't we?"

"We certainly do."

He stopped walking, pressed his hands around her face, and kissed her, a long, slow kiss. "It's so great to see you. When we get back to the house you'll meet my family. They're not like other people's families. It's all very heavy at the moment. I'll explain later. Right now I just want you near me. Is that okay with you?"

She nodded. It was fine with her. Thank God he was all right. Soon she had to warn him about Dukey, tell him the whole story. And when he knew, what then? Would he still want her? Or would that be it?

She sighed deeply. If they were going to have a relationship, the truth had to be told.

"There's my suitcase." She pointed out her Vuitton bag.

Nick signaled a porter, and they set off for the car.

Chapter 46

Mary Ann August left Enzio's room quietly. Outside his door was the suitcase she'd packed neatly with her possessions. She'd found her things where she'd left them and had encountered no problems getting past the guards. All she'd had to do was stroll through the grounds in her red bikini as if she still lived there.

She wasn't sure why she decided to shoot Enzio. It had all seemed so easy; the little gun he'd given her for her own protection was still in her jewelry case. And he was such a cold bastard. Leaving her in New York. Sending Alio along to take his turn. Shipping her off to a whorehouse in Los Angeles as if she were less than nothing. Keeping all her things.

Now that it was done she started to shake.

What if she couldn't get away?

What if someone *found* him before she could escape?

She hurried down the hallway, and to her horror, just as she was about to pass his wife's room, the door opened and the crazy woman called Rose appeared.

Rose Bassalino *never* left her room. Mary Ann had lived in the house for months, and she knew the door was *never* opened.

Rose stepped into the hallway, and they faced each other. She had wild, matted black hair, and penetrating, insane eyes.

Mary Ann shuddered as the woman smiled at her—a strange, faraway smile. And then Rose Bassalino lifted the knife she was carrying and, taking Mary Ann by surprise, plunged it into her stomach.

Mary Ann slid silently to the floor. Rose drew the long knife out of the girl's body and continued along the hallway until she reached Enzio's room.

He was asleep in bed, the covers drawn tightly around his chin.

Rose began to laugh as she plunged the knife into him.

Plunge, laugh, plunge, laugh.

It was the same knife he'd used so many years ago to murder Charles Cardwell.

A strange and wonderful justice.

Chapter 47

It was nearly five when Leroy parked his Mercedes some distance away from the Bassalino mansion. He was beginning to feel tired; it had been a long day.

Stepping from the car, he stretched, at the same time taking stock of his surroundings. There was no one around to observe him. He'd taken care of most of the work on his last trip.

Opening the trunk of his car, he took out a small canvas carryall, opened it, and scanned the contents. Finally satisfied, he set off for the house.

* * *

"Christ! We've been sitting here forever," Nick complained. "Goddamn traffic."

"Calm down," Lara said, squeezing his hand.

They were crawling along a three-lane highway, every lane slow-moving.

"It usually takes no more than fifteen minutes to the house," he said impatiently, lighting up a cigarette. "Today we'll be lucky to make it in an hour."

He knew he should have waited for Lara at the house; it was stupid to have left. Things could be moving, information might be coming through, and he should be there.

"It seems like there's some kind of accident up ahead," the driver said. "Looks like a bad one. Once we're past it'll be clear."

"Take the next turnoff," Nick instructed. "I know a shortcut." He squeezed her hand back. "We'll be there soon, baby."

Leroy strolled toward the gates of the Bassalino mansion, pausing several yards away.

One of the guards stepped out of the security gatehouse and watched him warily.

Very slowly Leroy reached into his blue canvas bag.

"Yeah?" the guard started to question, his hand tightening on a pistol stuck in his belt.

In one fluid movement Leroy produced a hand grenade from his bag, deftly removed the pin, and flung it at the guardhouse, throwing himself flat on the ground. Seconds later the earth shook from the explosion.

Leroy counted to five, jumped up, grabbed his bag, and ran past the flames into the grounds of the main house. Running fast, he dodged and weaved through the trees.

He could see the mansion. The front door was open, and men were racing out with guns drawn. Lots of dumb white motherfuckers. They didn't know what hit 'em.

Under the cover of the tall trees Leroy managed to get to the back of the house. Nobody spotted him. The assholes didn't even think to let the dogs loose. Even if they had, he was prepared.

Stealthily he made his way over to a back window. It took him less than a minute to dig up wires he'd buried on his last visit. Connect them, set the timer. Preparation. That was the secret. What a fucking brilliant scheme!

Get moving, he thought to himself. Never cut it too fine.

He started to run from the house, doing a fast countdown in his head.

Ten. Nine. Eight. Seven. Six.

Keep on running.

Five. Four. Three. Two. One. Zero.

POW! The first explosion, and, at intervals of five seconds, more explosions all around the house, just as he'd planned it.

Suddenly, with a leaden feeling in the pit of his stomach, he realized he'd made one fatal mistake. He realized it when he saw the pack of ferocious German shepherds heading in his direction.

His blue canvas bag. He'd left it on the ground by the back window, and in it was the fresh steak he'd brought to keep the dogs happy.

"Shit!" Leroy uttered.

It was the last word he ever spoke.

Chapter 48

Cass Long was alone when she saw the news on television.

Her first reaction was of an almost satisfied shock, until the full horror of the event overpowered her as television cameras hovered in a helicopter above the wreck that had once been the Bassalino mansion.

The scene was one of devastation. Fires were still burning, while police and firemen swarmed all over the place. A row of blanket-covered victims was lined up beside the swimming pool.

"It has not been established," the newscaster

said, "how many bodies are still to be recovered from the house. However, authorities seem certain there are more to come." The newscaster paused as further information was relayed to him. "It appears that a series of bombs were placed around the house, triggered to go off at short intervals. We will have more news on that later. The owner of the Miami mansion, Enzio Bassalino, was a well-known underworld figure in Chicago in the late twenties, along with his contemporaries Al Capone and Legs Diamond. In recent years, Mr. Bassalino has lived in seclusion and retirement at his house in Miami with—"

Cass clicked the television off. For a moment she stared at a framed photograph of Margaret hanging on the wall.

It was time to take up the work again. Time to go out in the world and try to achieve some of Margaret's goals.

Cass knew exactly who she could turn to.

Chapter 49

Lara would always remember the fear and the panic of that afternoon with Nick. They were less than minutes from the house when the explosions started.

"What is it?" she'd asked fearfully. There was a noise like long rumbling peals of thunder.

"Jesus Christ!" Nick yelled. "Move this fucking car!" he screamed at the driver.

As they drew closer they both saw smoke and flames coming from the house. "Stop!" Nick instructed urgently. "Turn the car around and take her back to the airport. Fast. Put her safely on a plane."

Jumping from the car, he ran toward the house. It was a nightmare scene.

"Nick!" she screamed after him. "Be careful. Oh, God! Be careful."

He didn't hear her; he'd vanished into the smoke, and the driver was already turning the car around and racing off in the other direction.

"Nick," she cried out in vain. "Oh, Nick, I love you."

The driver followed his instructions. He took her to the airport and put her on a plane to New York. She was too numb to argue.

When she arrived she went straight to Cass's apartment. Rio was already there.

"Have you seen the news?" Cass asked.

Lara held her breath. "What exactly happened?" She knew it was something terrible.

"Dukey scored," Rio said without emotion. "He had someone burn the Bassalino mansion down. They're all dead. So much for our efforts."

"Dead?" Lara asked blankly. "How do you know?"

"It's all over the television," Cass said grimly. "Nobody had a chance. The house was surrounded with explosives. It was a death trap."

Shortly after that Dukey arrived, smoking a big cigar. He smiled at everyone. "This is a celebration," he said triumphantly. "We did it my way."

"*Your* way," Rio said, her voice filled with disgust. "You make me want to throw up."

"Results," he boasted. "That's all that counts."

"You cold bastard!" Lara said, fighting back tears.

He puffed on his cigar. "Why don't you call me a *black* bastard—isn't that the kind of name-calling people like you do?"

"You've got no conscience."

"Oh, and I suppose you have? Fucking a guy is okay if it works out. But my way is shit."

"Your way is murder," Rio pointed out.

"They murdered Margaret," he countered.

"All those innocent people . . ." sighed Cass.

"Fuck it, girl," Dukey said. "Margaret was worth every one of them ten times over. An' let me tell you a little fact of life—there's nobody innocent involved with the Bassalinos."

Cass shook her head. "You don't understand, do you? Margaret wouldn't have approved of any of this. All she'd have wanted was for her work to be carried on."

"Get real, Cass. *I* wanted revenge. And *I* got it. Every one of those Bassalino bastards dead. Every mothafuckin' one."

"How do you know?" Lara asked flatly.

"Because *I* took care of it, sugar. I took care of it good."

Lara returned to her apartment. Nick was dead, and she was through crying. There were no more tears left. Why hadn't she warned him in time? It was all her fault.

She didn't know what she would do now. Everything seemed so hopeless.

When her phone rang she was tempted not to answer. It was probably Prince Alfredo, and she couldn't deal with him right now.

On the fourth ring she changed her mind. Listlessly she said, "Hello."

"Princess? Is that really you? Thank Christ you got out in time."

Relief and joy swept over her. "Nick! You're safe!"

"I can't talk. It's a mess here. I'm with the cops now. Jesus, Lara—my mother, father, my whole family . . ." He started to choke up.

"Let me fly back. I want to be with you."

"No. I'll call you again tomorrow. Just wait for me, sweetheart. You're all I've got."

"Nick . . . There are a lot of things I have to tell you . . ."

"Not now."

"When?"

"Soon, baby, soon."

* * *

She never did tell him. Somehow she couldn't summon the courage. He came to fetch her in New York, and they flew back to California together. A few days later they took off for Hawaii, where they were married in a simple private ceremony. The only person she confided in was Beth, safely back at the commune and happy to be reunited with her little girl and her boyfriend, Max.

"I don't know how it happened, but it did," Lara told her sister over the phone. "And I'm not telling the others," she added defiantly. "Let them find out for themselves."

Beth didn't lecture or judge. "The Bassalinos have been punished more than enough," she said quietly. "I hope you and Nick can find happiness."

"We will," Lara said confidently. "We're going to move to Italy and start over. Nick wants to, and so do I. When we're settled will you visit us?"

"You bet!" Beth replied.

Chapter 50

Bosco Sam and Dukey K. Williams met at the zoo.

"I ain't truckin' with you past those goddamn monkeys again," Bosco Sam complained. "I'm still smelling monkey piss every time I wear my damn coat."

Dukey laughed.

Bosco Sam glared.

"So, what's goin' on?" Dukey asked. "Lay it on me, bro', 'cos I gotta be at rehearsal two hours ago. Little blond number held me up."

"Dukey, boy, we had a deal."

"Right on. Ain't nobody arguing that fact."

Bosco Sam produced a Hershey bar from his coat pocket and carefully peeled off the wrapper. "Deal was I forget the two hundred thou, and you arrange the hit on the Bassalinos. Right?"

Dukey nodded.

"Okay, Frank Bassalino I give you. But the others? C'mon Dukey, who're you shittin'?"

"Hey, man—Enzio was the important one. Leroy did a great job."

"Leroy Jesus Bauls got his ass chewed off by a pack of fuckin' wild hounds. What was left of him his own mother wouldn't recognize. The cops showed me the photos. I got *very fine* connections with the police."

"So?"

"So the word is that Enzio was got at *before* the house blew. Someone shot him through the heart an' sliced him up with a butcher's knife —just for kicks. You gettin' the picture?"

Dukey licked his lips. "No, man, I'm not."

"Angelo Bassalino got his in a car wreck. Nick Bassalino's back in L.A. I reckon that still leaves you one hundred and fifty thousand in my debt."

"Don't fuckin' lay this shit on me, man," Dukey said angrily. "You can't possibly mean—"

"I'll tell you what," Bosco Sam interrupted.

"With interest we'll call it a straight two hundred thousand. Two days, my man. I'll give you two days. An' that's generous of me."

"Come on," Dukey groaned. "You're full of shit. This ain't fair!"

"Fair? I've been very fair with you. I don't have to tell you what happens next. Two days is generous."

"You fat fuck!" Dukey exclaimed. "You jealous asshole. You'll get your money."

Bosco Sam nodded. "Sure I will, Dukey boy. Cash. An' I want it by six o'clock tonight." Abruptly he shoved the rest of the chocolate bar in his mouth and walked away.

Dukey began to sweat.

There was no way he could get two hundred thousand together by six o'clock. No way.

Chapter 51

"The man who comes to you with his dick hanging out may want to make it with you, but does he want to work next to you? Does he want to see you get paid the same money for the same job he's doing? Hey—what about the guy in the street who undresses you with his eyes, fucks you with his mouth to his friends. Is he your equal, baby? Well? *Well?*"

The crowd of women, joined by a few males at the rock festival, screamed their agreement.

"Hey, sisters—you want to be put down by a race of male pigs forever? *Old* pigs with racist, chauvinistic, biased, old-fashioned views on *every* single thing that affects women in America today?

"To them we are pieces of ass. Look pretty, have the kids, but baby—stay home or you'd better stay quiet."

Rio Java was speaking between appearances of rock groups. With her frizzy purple hair and sequinned makeup she looked like a rock star herself.

In one year she had become as dedicated and intense as Margaret Lawrence Brown ever was. And her following was just as large. In fact, she attracted an even wider group of supporters than Margaret, as even the freaks liked her.

"One day I'm going to be president," she'd tell anyone who would listen. "And I'm going to expose the whole stinking, corrupt mess that politics represents.

"For a start," she told her friends, "I'm exposing that son of a bitch Larry Bolding. He ain't gonna be chasin' *nothin'* when *I* get through with him."

Larry Bolding, her ex-lover, the politician with the clean-cut image, elegant blond wife, and two perfect little kiddies, was running as a presidential candidate.

Rio held both arms straight up above her purple hair and made fists of her hands.

"Strike out, sisters!" she shouted. "Strike out!! We are going to get what we want. We are going to be EQUAL in every way!"

The crowd whistled and screamed approval.

Rio felt the bullet hit her. She stood very still. She smiled. And the crowd spread out before her whistled and stamped and screamed.

"Strike out!" Rio managed. But then the blood bubbled up her throat and out of her mouth in one life-taking gush.

Chapter 52

The house in Connecticut could only be approached by passing through electric gates and then undergoing the scrutiny of two uniformed guards with pistols stuck casually in their belts.

Dickson Grade passed this scrutiny easily. He was a precise-looking man in a dark business suit. He wore rimless glasses on small brown eyes, and his hair was combed neatly back.

He approached the big house, holding a slim leather briefcase tightly by his side.

A uniformed maid answered his ring. "Good

afternoon, Mr. Grade, sir," she said respectfully. "Mr. Bolding is out by the pool."

Dickson Grade nodded, making his way through the house to the patio, which led out to an Olympic-size swimming pool.

Susan Bolding greeted him. She was a most attractive woman, with straight fair hair pulled firmly back in a French twist. Her shapely figure was concealed beneath a loose silk shirt and tailored white trousers.

"Hello, Dick." She smiled, kissing him lightly on the cheek. "What can I get you? A drink? Tea? Coffee?"

Dickson smiled politely. He found Larry Bolding's wife extremely appealing, but when you were Larry Bolding's personal assistant you sat on thoughts like that and did nothing about them.

"Coffee, please, Susan. Where is Larry?"

"Exploring the garden in search of weeds, I think. Honestly, Sunday is the only day he gets time to relax. And you know how he loves his garden."

"I'll go find him."

Dickson walked down a side path until he discovered Larry Bolding playing catch on the grass with his children.

They greeted each other, and then Larry sent the children off to find Mommy. He was a tall, clean-cut man in his early forties. Craggy good looks combined nicely with a deep, masculine voice and a politician's firm handshake.

"Everything is under control," Dickson said. "A perfect operation."

Larry Bolding glanced around to make perfectly sure they were alone. "Is she—dead?" he asked in a low voice.

Dickson nodded. "And nothing to connect it to us. You're in the clear. Oh, and rest assured, the right people will be dealing with her personal effects."

Larry Bolding sighed and patted Dickson on the shoulder. "It was the only way, wasn't it?" he questioned.

Dickson Grade nodded agreement. "The only way."

THE FABULOUS HEROINE OF *CHANCES* RETURNS . . . SHE'S A HOT-BLOODED BEAUTY, IN LOVE WITH POWER, HUNGRY FOR PLEASURE . . . WILD, NOTORIOUS, TROUBLE . . . SHE'S . . .

Lucky

With the sensual grace of a panther, Lucky Santangelo prowled her Las Vegas casino, restless, ready, eager for action. That night began a dazzling odyssey, filled with dangerous passion and sun-drenched sex, sadistic vengeance and breathless suspense.

From the decadent luxury of California, to Paris, New York and a private Greek island, Lucky fought for her father's honor, for ruthless triumph, for the wild card of a fabulous love. Her rivals: an ice-cold Hollywood wife . . . a much-married heiress strung out on cocaine . . . a jaded magnate hooked on power . . . a crazed hoodlum lusting for murder. But Lucky was a gambler and a lover, a woman who ruled her empire and pursued her man with the potent Santangelo strength . . . her way, on her terms, whatever the odds.

Jackie Collins tops the sensational success of *Hollywood Wives* and *Chances* with *LUCKY*, ". . . so hot it will have to be printed on asbestos."

—Liz Smith, *New York Daily News*

Jackie Collins

The World Is Full Of Married Men

SUCCULENT STARLETS READY TO MAKE IT . . . RICH MOGULS HUNGRY FOR HOTTER PLEASURES . . . ON THE CASTING COUCH, AT LAVISH PARTIES, IN PLUSH HOTEL SUITES . . .

The World Is Full Of Married Men

Jackie Collins bares the burning ambitions, the vicious power-plays, the sexual double-dealings of the entertainment world . . . where wives wait for husbands who never come, and luscious models pay more than their dues . . . where talent and drive take you just so far, but sex can take you all the way.

FROM DAZZLING LAS VEGAS TO LONDON'S WILD DISCOS, FROM ATHENS TO HOLLYWOOD, JACKIE COLLINS REVEALS IT ALL . . .

The Bitch

Fontaine Khaled reigns over the jet set, a sensational beauty, hard as diamonds, rich as a queen. Women envy her, men adore her, hustlers cruise her, everyone wants a piece of . . .

The Bitch

She'd dropped a rich Arab for her latest thrill—a private stable of husky studs, erotic delights in chauffeured limousines, hot sex on black satin sheets. As long as the money lasts, she'll always be . . .

The Bitch

But a fast-moving, hard-gambling Greek with boudoir eyes and a murderous charm seduces her into a night of incredible passion. Nico has desperate reasons of his own to win, to possess, to use . . .

The Bitch

Jackie Collins

Sinners

STARS AND STUDS, HOOKERS AND HOPEFULS, HOLLYWOOD'S RICH, BEAUTIFUL, BRILLIANT AND DEPRAVED—JACKIE COLLINS BARES ALL THEIR SECRETS!

Sinners

Hollywood—glittering premieres, dazzling movie sets, fabulous parties, plush love-nests hidden in Malibu and Beverly Hills. Behind the gorgeous playgrounds of the rich and renowned lies a jungle of lust and perversity, greed and ambition, love and danger—where survival is all, and innocence is a role nobody plays for long.

Jackie Collins uncovers all the sex, all the scandals, all the private obsessions of filmland's famous in the shocking, passionate world of . . .

Sinners

FEEL THE HUNGER,
THE BEAT, THE HEAT
ROCK STAR BURNS . . .

Rock Star

KRIS PHOENIX: the wild English rocker with the raunchy strut, spiky hair and dazzling blue eyes . . . BOBBY MONDELLA: the black king of throbbing soul with the sensuous moves and the sexy voice . . . RAFEALLA: the dark, exotic beauty with every reason to sing the blues.

They've got it all, and life in the fast lane is hot. Parties, booze, drugs, power and sex. But the bright lights can't erase the price they paid on the raw, lonely road to the top . . .

Now a tough record magnate and his icy wife bring the three stars together in concert. Onstage at a plush California estate, their fates collide at last. And as the music blasts to a climax, one man's desperate, secret vendetta will trap Kris, Rafealla and Bobby in its sudden, murderous heat.

"COLLINS COMES THROUGH . . . WITH LOADS OF SEX AND INTRIGUE . . . AN UNEXPECTED AND SATISFYING CLIMAX . . . FANS WILL ADORE *ROCK STAR.*" —United Press International

"IF YOU PICK UP THIS BOOK, YOU WON'T PUT IT DOWN . . . COLLINS FANS WILL GOBBLE UP *ROCK STAR.*" —*Vogue*

Jackie Collins

Hollywood Wives

"THE PAGES SIMPLY THROB WITH THE JUNGLE BEAT OF MATING AND THE STRANGE TRIBAL RITES OF THE WOMEN BEHIND THE MEN WHO MAKE THE MOVIES." *—Los Angeles Magazine*

From Rodeo Drive to Malibu to Palm Springs, nobody knows the glittering world of love, lust and betrayal like Jackie Collins. It's her world . . . the glamorous, sinful, heaven-on-earth of . . .

Hollywood Wives

The fabulous beauties, famous and infamous, tough, tan, terrific—married to success, divorced from care, flirting with scandal. They bewitch their men with sensuous cunning, naked and greedy under silk sheets, hungry to devour every new superstud. Supremely wealthy, utterly powerful, endlessly passionate, totally ruthless—the shameless women whose every shocking secret Jackie Collins reveals from the inside out . . .

Hollywood Wives

Jackie Collins

Hollywood Husbands

HOLLYWOOD HUSBANDS ARE HOT . . .
HOLLYWOOD HUSBANDS ARE SEXY . . .
HOLLYWOOD HUSBANDS GO ALL THE WAY . . .

In Ferraris and Rolls-Royces, they cruise the town, high on the sweet taste of power. At champagne-drenched parties and fabulous premieres, they get the best deals and the most gorgeous women, while their wives spend their money as fast as they can.

Hollywood Husbands

A television king, a studio magnate, a stud superstar. Expensive divorces and sizzling, dangerous affairs make them hungry for more exotic conquests. Bronzed, muscled, savvy, successful, they attract new lovers with dazzling ease . . .

Always rivals, three friends who made it, they'll play the star game for the highest stakes. They'll survive every scandal, devour every sensation, while one woman burns with the deadly heat of a cunning, depraved revenge . . .

"JACKIE COLLINS IS HOLLYWOOD'S UNDISPUTED SCHEHERAZADE OF THE STARS."

—*New York Post*